To Whom It May Concern,

Marriage? It's not for someone like me.

I've spent years recklessly pursuing a career as an award-winning television news correspondent. My work is my life, my family, my motivation and my recreation. I've tried to be content with that. As the ne'er-do-well younger son of a household that prides itself on perfection, I've learned to accept my limitations.

There have been times when I've wished for more. A wife, a family to welcome me home when I've been away on assignment. But it would take a very special woman to see beneath the playboy facade I've assumed for so long. If such a paragon really does exist, how could I ever tell her about my dishonorable past?

Tristan Parrish

Please address questions and book requests to: Harlequin Reader Service
U.S.: 3010 Walden Ave., P.O. Box 1325, Buffalo, NY 14269
Canadian: P.O. Box 609, Fort Erie, Ont. L2A 5X3

Reluctant Grooms

GINA WILKINS
DESIGNS ON LOVE

Harlequin Books

TORONTO • NEW YORK • LONDON
AMSTERDAM • PARIS • SYDNEY • HAMBURG
STOCKHOLM • ATHENS • TOKYO • MILAN
MADRID • WARSAW • BUDAPEST • AUCKLAND

HARLEQUIN BOOKS
225 Duncan Mill Road, Don Mills,
Ontario, Canada M3B 3K9

ISBN 0-373-30103-0

DESIGNS ON LOVE

Copyright © 1992 by Gina Wilkins

Celebrity Wedding Certificates published by permission of
Donald Ray Pounders from *Celebrity Wedding Ceremonies*.

Printed in U.S.A.

A Letter from the Author

Dear Reader,

There were so many elements of *Designs on Love* that made it a joy for me to write: the dashing, leather-jacketed television news correspondent; the prim and proper "good girl" who tries for once in her life to be wicked; their eclectic collection of friends; and all those gorgeous fairy-tale wedding gowns that I found in the pages of bridal magazines while doing my research. Tristan and Devon were a very special couple to me.

I never grow tired of celebrating the power of love in my books. As my own twentieth wedding anniversary approaches, I still fully believe in happily-ever-after!

Sincerely,

Gina Wilkins

For Donna—
With thanks for the menu,
and for stepping in the wallpaper paste.
I warned you I'd use it.

Prologue

"YOU'RE SUCH A GOOD GIRL, Devon," said her grandmother as Devon lovingly adjusted Grammie's shawl over frail shoulders.

Such a good girl. Devon winced. She was twenty-eight years old, but to her mother and Grammie she'd always be their little girl. Their *good* little girl. But, then, why should they think of her any differently? That's exactly what she'd always been for them, she reflected wryly.

She glanced up to find her younger sister watching her mockingly. If Devon was the good girl, Brandy would always be the mischief maker, the scamp. At twenty-four Brandy was gorgeous, extroverted and adventurous. All her life Devon had heard her mother asking, "What are we going to do with Brandy? Thank *goodness* Devon's such a good girl."

"*Now* can we open our presents?" Brandy asked impatiently. "I do have a date this evening, you know. I still don't understand why we can't open presents on Christmas Eve or Christmas morning like everyone else in the world. Why do we have to wait until after Christmas dinner?"

"Because that's the way we've always done it, Brandy," Grammie answered firmly, as if no other explanation were needed.

And, Devon thought with a secret grin, no other explanation *was* needed. Tradition was a powerful influence in the Fleming household. For as far back as Devon could remember, Grammie had lived with them in this tiny frame house in rural Georgia. Devon had been only eight and Brandy four when their father had died. Fortunately for everyone involved, Alice Fleming had gotten along beautifully with her mother-in-law. Both were loving, old-fashioned, gentle-natured women who stubbornly resisted change in any form; only with great reluctance did they allow Devon and Brandy to grow up and begin their own lives.

Devon adored her mother and grandmother, but had seized the first opportunity to move to Atlanta, some forty minutes away—near enough to keep a close eye on the older women, far enough to maintain some distance from their rather obsessive affection. Devon's bid for independence had been a subtle one, unlike Brandy's which had involved openly rebelling against the sometimes-smothering bonds of family almost since learning to walk.

"Don't be so impatient, Brandy," Alice told her younger daughter with a smile of fond exasperation. "Of course we'll open presents now, unless— Did anyone want anything else to eat or drink first?"

Devon and Brandy groaned in unison, a rare moment of consensus between the two. "Believe me, Mom, we couldn't possibly eat another bite," Devon assured her.

Alice beamed in satisfaction. "Then who wants to pass out the presents?"

Devon and Brandy looked at each other in a silent battle of wills. Brandy finally sighed and tossed her heavy blond-streaked mane away from her dramatically made-up face. "All right, *I'll* do it. At least it won't take as long that way. Devon always wants to wait for each present to be opened and admired before she hands out the next one."

Thanks to Brandy's no-nonsense method of distributing packages, it was only a short time later when, surrounded by the blouses and scarves and books and hand-knit items she traditionally received from her family, Devon opened her last gift, which was from her mother. "Oh, this is lovely, Mom. And it looks so warm. Thank you," she said, lifting the snow-white brushed-cotton nightgown from the box, her lips curving upward at the almost virginal styling of the high-necked, long-sleeved garment.

Her mother knew, of course, that Devon liked warm, comfortable nightwear. Devon wondered if Alice didn't honestly believe her elder daughter was still a virgin, despite a two-year engagement that had ended four years before, when her fiancé had finally decided he and Devon weren't suited. Devon's reaction once she'd gotten over the pain of her severely bruised pride had been overwhelming relief at finding herself free to pursue the dream she'd always had of operating her own business as a dress designer—something that would have been denied her as Wade Carleton's dutiful "corporate" wife.

"Oh wow, Mom, this is gorgeous! And so naughty. Aren't you ashamed of yourself?" Brandy teased, holding up her own nightgown. Like Devon's, Brandy's gown was white. Unlike Devon's, this one was delectably sexy, a froth of lace and almost-sheer silk.

Her lined cheeks suspiciously pink, Alice cleared her throat. "I found it on a half-price rack at J. C. Penney's," she admitted. "It was terribly expensive originally, but it was such a good buy—and it did look like something you'd like."

Brandy laughed and air-kissed her mother's cheek. "I love it. Thanks, Mom."

Devon realized her fingers had clenched into her own soft, sweet nightgown tightly enough to crumple the fabric. Very carefully she loosened them and folded the garment back into its box. It was a lovely gown, she reminded herself sternly. *Such a sweet gown for such a good girl*, a voice inside her mocked.

Frowning, Devon busied herself gathering scraps of paper and ribbon, wondering what in the world had come over her today. It was Christmas and she was with her family, whom she loved dearly. So why did she feel that there was something missing from her safe, productive, comfortably predictable life?

DEVON GLANCED AT HER watch as she paced the small parlor she'd converted into an office for client consultations. Sara Archer was almost ten minutes late. She hoped Sara hadn't forgotten their appointment to approve the final sketches for Sara's wedding gown. Having known the prospective bride for several years, Devon was aware that the young woman was hopelessly disorganized, despite her undeniable intelligence.

It was impossible to know Sara Archer and not love her. Devon was rapidly learning that it was almost as impossible to refuse her anything, once she had her mind set. The peplum on her wedding dress, for example. Sara had insisted she wanted one just below the waistline of the basque bodice. Devon had done her best to blend the peplum with the other features Sara had requested, but she wasn't happy about the final look. She'd worked successfully with peplums before, even liked them most of the time, but on the style of gown Sara had chosen, it was wrong. Devon had made a second sketch of the dress without a peplum, hoping Sara would see the improvement. If not— Well, Devon's business was to create wedding gowns that pleased the brides, not her own taste.

No, what worried her was Sara's single-minded determination to find a wife for her father, whom she was quite sure would be desperately lonely after the wedding. Devon had considered the matchmaking scheme amusing—until she'd realized that Sara had picked *her* as a prospective stepmother. Devon had tried to resist, but somehow she had a dinner date with Neal Archer Friday night. She wondered if for Neal, too, it had been a matter of being unable to hold out against his daughter.

Though she had only seen him a couple of times, Devon thought Neal was very nice. He was attractive, charming, successful, polite. Her mother and grandmother would adore him, she reflected with a sigh. Exactly the type of man they had in mind for Devon. So why didn't her pulse race when Neal smiled at her? And why wasn't she counting the hours until the dinner date tomorrow evening? Or was she being hopelessly naive to expect ever to have those romantic, fairy-tale feelings?

Exasperated by her uncharacteristic fancifulness, Devon ordered herself to concentrate on her work. What was with her lately, anyway? She wondered if her sudden longing for romance had anything to do with her best friend's recently announced engagement.

Liz Archer was a wedding consultant whom Devon had met several years earlier through their related work. They and a talented young photographer, Holly Baldwin, had been friends ever since. All of them single, they'd formed a close threesome, sharing frequent dinners and long, cozy gossip sessions. Liz, who was very close to her niece, had brought Sara along on several of their outings, making Sara an honorary niece to Devon and Holly.

And now Liz, too, was engaged. After knowing Chance Cassidy only a month—most of that time spent arguing about the upcoming wedding between Liz's niece and Chance's younger brother—Liz had fallen in love with the stubborn construction-company owner. They would be married in the spring and then Liz would be moving to Chance's home in Birmingham. Happiness had radiated from her in almost-visible waves when she'd broken the news to her friends. Holly and Devon were both frankly envious, though Devon had hidden her emotions better than bluntly outspoken Holly.

Devon told herself it was petty to envy a dear friend's happiness. She looked again at her watch, wondering what was keeping Sara. She knew Sara was excited about seeing her wedding-gown sketches and wouldn't deliberately miss the appointment. Devon wished the young woman would hurry so that she could concentrate on her work and not on her mixed emotions about the upcoming dinner date with Neal Archer.

TRISTAN PARRISH GUIDED his beloved little sports car slowly along crowded University Avenue, his eyes searching the sidewalks. His mouth tilted into a smile when he spotted the pretty brunette waving to him from beside a wrought-iron lamppost. He promptly pulled over to the curb.

"Thanks so much for the lift, Tristan. I don't know what I would have done if I hadn't tracked you down. I don't have enough money on me for cab fare and Daddy was in a meeting and Phillip's taking an exam and I *promised* Devon I'd be at her house at eleven and here it is ten minutes till and that damn—um—darned car of mine won't start *again*."

Accustomed to Sara's free-form chatter, Tristan deciphered the tirade easily enough. "Neal warned you it wasn't exactly a dependable vehicle, particularly in cold weather. But you had your heart set on it. Do up your belt, love."

Sara sighed and belted herself in. "It's just such a pretty car. *You* have an old classic, Tristan. Why doesn't yours spend half its time in the shop?"

"Because Bessie and I have an understanding, don't we, sweet?" He patted the dash with a fond hand. "I provide unlimited quarts of oil and she takes me where I want to go. It's a mutually satisfying relationship."

"Well, *I* think it's because all cars are female and there isn't a female alive who can resist your charm," Sara teased, leaning over to kiss his cheek with easy familiarity.

He chuckled and glanced over his shoulder for a break in traffic. "Present company excluded, of course."

"Oh, no, I'm just as gullible as the rest of them," she assured him solemnly.

"Then why are you marrying Phillip, when I've been waiting years for you to grow up?" he demanded with mock severity.

She laughed and tossed her head, looking so young and happy that Tristan felt suddenly much older than his thirty-eight years. God, had he ever been this young, even at twenty?

"I know better than that," Sara said, smiling across the console at him. "If any woman tried to put a ring on your finger, you'd run as far and as fast as your adventure-loving legs would carry you. Daddy warned me about you when I turned twelve and developed my first major crush on you."

"Oh, really? And just what did your father say about me?"

"That you were a walking heartache. Love 'em and leave 'em. The more, the merrier," Sara answered bluntly. "I thought that only made you more romantic and exciting, of course, but I stopped daydreaming about marrying you. And, besides, you used to give me piggyback rides."

Tristan winced and felt ten more years settle upon him. Much more of Sara's brand of candor and he'd be needing a cane to get out of his car, he thought ruefully. "Exactly where is it that I'm taking you, Sara?" he asked, deliberately changing the subject.

"Oh, sorry." She quickly gave him directions. "Devon works out of her house," she explained. "She's designing my wedding gown. I'm going today to approve the preliminary design. I promise it will only take a few minutes, but if you're in a hurry, you can just drop me off there and I can get a cab home."

"I thought you said you didn't have cab fare."

She gave him her sweetest smile. "I don't. I had to contribute everything I had with me for a friend's birthday present this morning."

He chuckled and shook his head. "Something tells me it will be cheaper for me if I simply wait there for you. Not that I expect this process to take 'only a few minutes,' you understand. Fortunately, I happen to be free for the entire afternoon."

"Good. Then you can take me for ice cream afterward. It's been ages since we visited our favorite ice-cream parlor."

"That's what I love most about you, Sara. You're so sweetly shy and undemanding."

She only laughed and patted his arm. Exactly as she would any amusing old gentleman's, Tristan reflected. Maybe he *should* start shopping for an attractive cane.

THE DOORBELL RANG twenty minutes after Sara was to have arrived. Relieved, Devon glanced at the sketches spread over the round oak table she used for client meetings and automatically smoothed her loosely styled, just-longer-than-shoulder-length hair as she moved to answer the summons.

The smile she'd worn for Sara froze on her face when she saw the man accompanying Liz's niece. He was tall, with gold-tipped blond hair, blue eyes, a deep tan— Heavens, he was *gorgeous!* He smiled at her and her lungs convulsed. Now *this* was a man who could make even a "good girl's" pulse race!

"Hi, Devon! I'm so sorry I'm late, but my car wouldn't start. It's the most exasperating thing. Oh, this is Daddy's friend, Tristan. You probably recognize him," Sara said airily, sweeping past Devon with a wave over her shoulder at the man following her.

Tristan's smile deepened ruefully. "Sara has an over-inflated estimation of my celebrity," he apologized in a deliciously British accent. "It's left to me to introduce myself. I'm—"

"Tristan Parrish, the television-news reporter," Devon finished for him, smiling as she offered her hand. "Sara's estimation wasn't exaggerated, after all. I recognized you immediately. I'm Devon Fleming, by the way."

Tristan's eyebrow rose in a gesture worthy of any movie heartthrob as he took her hand. Pure male appreciation gleamed in his blue eyes when he studied her face. Devon tried to fight down a blush, knowing he probably looked at every woman over eighteen and under eighty in just this way. "I'm delighted to meet you, Devon Fleming," he said. "And just how big is Mr. Fleming?"

Devon blinked; Sara laughed. "Honestly, Tristan, don't you ever stop?" she demanded in feigned exasperation. "Don't listen to a word he says, Devon. The man is a hopeless flirt."

"Never hopeless, Sara," he corrected, still holding Devon's hand. "Always hopeful." And then, as if to make a point, he stroked his thumb slowly across Devon's palm as he released her, making shivers of sensation course all the way up her arm, while Sara laughed again at his obvious technique.

Devon's fingers curled into her still-tingling palm. Her smile felt strained. "Maybe we'd better look at the sketches," she suggested, turning toward the worktable. And then some unknown impulse made her glance back over her shoulder at Tristan. "And, by the way, there *is* no Mr. Fleming."

She thought he looked pleased, though she turned away too quickly to tell for certain.

"They're beautiful, Devon! Absolutely beautiful," Sara exclaimed a few minutes later. "Exactly what I always dreamed of. What do you think, Tristan? You know more about women's clothes than any other man I know."

Tristan grimaced reprovingly at the excited young woman before examining the sketches. For some strange reason, Devon found herself holding her breath as she awaited his opinion. In exasperation, she asked herself why it should matter. She'd designed the dress for Sara's approval, not this man's.

He studied the sketches carefully, all of them, making Devon's tension climb. And then he pointed out one sheet to Sara. "I like it much better this way."

Sara bit her lip. "Really? You like it best without the peplum?"

"Quite."

Sara sighed. "So does Devon. But I think it's kind of cute. I saw one like it in a bridal magazine and I—"

"Then by all means keep the peplum," Tristan replied equably, dropping his hand. "The dress should please you, after all. It really doesn't matter whether— Well, never mind."

"What doesn't matter?" Sara demanded apprehensively.

"Not to worry, love. You have a lovely figure," Tristan assured her affectionately. "Of course, the ruffle just there will add a few visual inches to your backside, but certainly everyone will know that it's only the dress. And if *you* like it, that's all that really matters, isn't it?"

Devon bit the inside of her lip against a smile at the horrified expression on Sara's pretty face. "The peplum will make my bottom look bigger?" She turned immediately to Devon. "Do you think so, too?"

Devon shrugged delicately. "Maybe a little. But you really do have a nice shape, Sara. And as you said, it is a very popular style, so if you want it—"

"No. Leave it off. Please, Devon, I've changed my mind."

Devon couldn't quite meet Tristan's gaze, though she knew he was watching her with amusement shining in his almost-silvery blue eyes. "No problem," she promised Sara gently. "We'll leave it off. Maybe you'd like a small bow on the lower back, just at the top of the skirt? The way I've sketched it here," she added, reaching for another sheet of drawing paper.

"Yes, I like that," Sara agreed immediately. And then she glanced warily at Tristan. "Um—Tristan?"

"It's a beautiful dress," he assured both of them. "And the bow is the perfect accent."

Sara smiled in obvious relief. It annoyed Devon that she felt the same way.

"We should be ready for a first fitting early next month," she told her client, gathering the sketches into a neat pile. "Why don't I call you then and set up an appointment? We'll discuss your attendants' dresses, as well."

"That will be fine," Sara said. "See, Tristan? I told you this wouldn't take long."

"I find myself disappointed," Tristan murmured, smiling at Devon.

Sara rolled her eyes. "Didn't I tell you he never stops? Come on, Tristan, stuff your libido into your pocket and let's go have that ice cream you offered me."

"*I* offered?" he repeated skeptically, though he followed Sara obediently to the door. He glanced around Devon's house as they left the parlor office and walked through her living room to the front door. "You've a nice place here," he commented, studying her simple, tastefully blended decor.

She thought of the two bedrooms littered with fabric, beads, pattern papers, lace, sewing machines, and the other tools of her trade. She could imagine his shock at the contrast between this room she kept immaculate for visitors and the controlled chaos of her work space. Even the master bedroom was a disaster at the moment, since she'd had a sudden urge to redecorate after returning home from Christmas with her family. For some reason she'd grown tired of the rather prim ruffles and lace and had decided to modernize. She'd taken down the eyelet curtains and the old-fashioned prints and stripped the rosebud wallpaper, but the demands of her work had prevented her from making further progress in the past week.

She thanked Tristan for his compliment and opened the front door.

Tristan hesitated on his way out. "Would you join us for ice cream?"

Devon smiled and shook her head. "Thank you, but I can't. I have another client due in an hour for a first consultation."

"We'll clear out of your way, then." He extended his hand. "It was very nice to meet you, Devon Fleming. We'll see each other again."

She placed her hand in his. "Maybe we will," she agreed. His fingers closed around hers and, as she had earlier when he'd taken her hand in his, she reacted in a distinctly physical way. She couldn't remember ever experiencing these odd tingles of sensation—not from a mere touch of hands. But then, she'd never met a man quite like Tristan Parrish before. She suspected that Sara's warnings of his success with women were well justified.

"Count on it," he responded. He lifted her hand and brushed his mouth lightly over her knuckles in what would have been a meaningless affectation from any other man. Tristan held her gaze with his, making the gesture all too significant. And then he released her and turned to Sara with a blinding smile. "Let's go, shall we?"

Hearing Sara's laughter and chatter fading down the walk, Devon closed the door and leaned weakly against it, staring at her hand as if she'd never seen it before— as if her knuckles should bear some visible evidence that they'd been touched by Tristan's lips.

"Wow!" she breathed as the sound of his car engine died away. "Now *that* is the kind of man Mom and Grammie always warned me to stay away from."

Which, of course, only made him all the more fascinating.

—————— **2** ——————

TRISTAN WAITED UNTIL Sara was seated behind a Hot Fudge Banana Nut Fantasy before saying, "She's not married?"

Sara dipped a spoon into her ice cream and shook her head. "No. Never has been. She and Aunt Liz are good friends."

"Are they?"

"Mmm. Have been for several years. I think they met through business. Liz always recommends Devon's work whenever a future bride wants a specially designed gown or attendants' dresses. She's fabulous."

Tristan feigned interest in his small bowl of lime sherbet. "She sews these dresses herself?"

"She can, but she usually concentrates on the designs. She has people who work for her who do the actual sewing. She rents a loft downtown where her employees work. I've seen it. It's fascinating—half a dozen sewing machines, big worktables, gorgeous fabrics everywhere. Devon checks in there a couple of times a day, I think, though she works primarily out of her home."

"She must be quite successful to afford hired seamstresses."

"Oh, she is. She's made a name for herself, here in Atlanta and all over Georgia. Several wedding boutiques across the state and in two neighboring states carry her gowns in their lines. She even designed an evening gown for Miss Georgia to wear in the last Miss America pageant. *Flair* magazine did a three-page article on her."

Tristan had always admired clever, successful businesswomen. He thought of the more obvious things he admired about Devon Fleming—her beautiful heart-shaped face, her glossy honey-brown hair, her golden brown eyes, her slender figure. She was thinner than the women he was usually attracted to, but her graceful, willowy shape suited her dainty features and delicate peach-toned coloring. Her tiny waist and slim hips had only emphasized the full, firm contours of her surprisingly generous bustline.

"I think she and Daddy will make a great couple, don't you?" Sara asked before spooning a small mound of ice cream and bananas into her mouth.

Tristan set his own spoon down abruptly. "Devon and Neal?" he asked carefully. "What do you mean?"

"They have a date tomorrow night," Sara answered confidingly. "I sort of arranged it, but they seemed agreeable enough. I'm hoping for another wedding in the near future—theirs."

Tristan winced and pushed his unfinished sherbet away, suddenly feeling rather sick. Pleasant, half-formed plans to further his acquaintance with the lovely Devon dissolved before his eyes. "A wedding," he repeated, his voice hollow.

Sara had the grace to blush. "Well, maybe I'm being a little optimistic," she admitted. "After all, they haven't even had a first date yet. But I think they'd make a great couple. Aunt Liz agrees with me. Now all we have to do is throw them together a couple of times and see if we're right."

And then she cocked her head and looked at Tristan closely. "What's the matter? You don't approve? You think Daddy and Devon are wrong for each other?"

Tristan sighed glumly. "No, they'll probably make a very nice couple," he conceded reluctantly. "Quite suitable."

Sara smiled suddenly. "You were going to ask her out, weren't you?"

"The thought had crossed my mind."

She patted his hand. "Sorry I spoiled your plans. But I'm hoping this date between Daddy and Devon will lead to something permanent. And it's not as if *you're* interested in marriage or commitment or anything serious, is it, Tristan?"

He managed a smile, thinking bitterly of how his family would scoff at the very idea of their irresponsible younger son settling down with a respectable woman. "Of course not. Think of my reputation."

"I *am* thinking of it," she assured him. "And I'm confident that I'm doing Devon a favor to discourage you from chasing after her. She's kind of old-fashioned, you know? Conservative. Not your usual type."

It had been a most illuminating afternoon. Tristan had learned that his best friend's daughter regarded him as little more than an aging roué out to seduce anything in a skirt. He was beginning to wish he hadn't been home when she'd called.

He looked at his watch. "I'm afraid we're going to have to hurry, Sara. I'm attending the governor's press conference this evening and I need to go over my notes."

"I thought you were on vacation this week and next."

"So I am. But I have a few questions I'd like to ask the governor about this new tax package he's proposing."

Sara took another quick bite of her nearly finished ice cream. "At least there won't be bullets flying over your head during this assignment," she commented when she'd swallowed. "I was so nervous watching you cover that military coup last week. Must you pursue your stories with quite so much dedication, Tristan? I mean, I'm sure you'll get another Pulitzer, but even your producers were aghast at some of the risks you took. Daddy was ready to strangle you for being so reckless."

Tristan groaned. Neal had made his opinion of Tristan's coverage of the coup quite clear. He'd implied that Tristan should take the anchor job he'd been offered and leave the location work to the younger reporters. Tristan had reminded Neal, of course, that Neal was two years older, but Neal had retorted that his work was safely behind a desk—as Tristan's should be. This was really all he needed today, Tristan thought glumly. Another reminder of the passing years.

"Unless you'd like another ice cream, Sara, we really should be going," he said with another meaningful glance at his watch, more than ready for the afternoon to end.

She looked longingly at her empty bowl as she reached for her purse and stood. "No—" she sighed "—I'd better not. Someone recently pointed out that my bottom isn't exactly tiny."

Tristan eyed her firm derriere with a lifted eyebrow. "Perhaps you shouldn't," he told her with a smile.

"Tristan!" she wailed, punching his arm as they walked out of the ice-cream parlor. "What a rotten thing to say. And I thought you were such a skilled ladies' man."

He grinned and opened his car door for her, then spent the next twenty minutes reassuring her that she was absolutely perfect and shouldn't lose one enchanting pound. She seemed quite satisfied by the time he dropped her off at the home she shared with her father in one of Atlanta's most exclusive neighborhoods. Again claiming the need to review his notes, Tristan brushed off her thanks for the rescue and the ice cream and declined her invitation to come in for a drink.

As he drove away, he found himself thinking again of Devon Fleming. Thinking that she and Neal probably would make a nice couple. And wishing he believed otherwise.

BENT OVER A WORKTABLE on which she was altering a pattern piece to fit her newest design, Devon gave only half her attention to the television playing in one corner of the room. She had it on for the noise, mostly, though she'd turned it to the cable news channel for live coverage of a press conference with the governor.

She frowned over a particularly difficult alteration, then nearly ruined the piece entirely when a familiar British-accented voice suddenly claimed her full attention. She set down her scissors and moved closer to the small-screen portable TV. The camera focused on Tristan as he asked his question.

"Isn't it true that the lower and middle classes will be bearing the heaviest tax burden if this new tax package goes into effect?" he demanded. "And what about the tax cuts you're considering for the larger corporations? How will those reductions benefit the general public, who will be even more heavily taxed this year?"

Devon had to smile at the fancy political footwork that followed Tristan's cutting inquiries. She wondered if it would bother Neal Archer that his best friend was publicly questioning tax cuts to large corporations such as Neal's. Obviously Tristan didn't allow his personal connections to interfere with his job.

Devon had always admired Tristan's work. Even before she'd met him, she'd found herself watching for his reports, had chewed her nails in apprehension when he reported from the center of violent confrontations. She'd watched him broadcast from Panama, Beijing, Bogotá, Belfast, Jordan, Saudi Arabia, the West Bank. She'd seen him dodge bullets, missiles and flying fists. And she'd admired his courageous pursuit of the news, even as she'd wondered how those who cared for him felt about watching him place himself in danger again and again in pursuit of a story.

Staring at the television long after another reporter had taken over the questioning, Devon sighed as she thought of how totally mismatched she would be with a man like Tristan Parrish. He was reckless, cosmopolitan, dangerously charming, determinedly footloose. He'd made a lighthearted pass at her that afternoon, but she told herself not to put much stock in that. Making passes probably came as easily to him as breathing. She'd be an idiot to take him seriously.

No, she was much more suited to a man like Neal Archer. Nice, polite, hardworking, settled. Safe. Tristan would be more interested in a woman like Brandy, who was as reckless and free spirited as he was.

With another long sigh, Devon turned back to her pattern, her attention focused fiercely on the design of another woman's wedding gown.

IT WAS MIDMORNING Friday and Tristan was still in bed, though he'd been awake for nearly half an hour. Truth was, there wasn't much reason to get up, he thought gloomily, one arm behind his head as he stared at the ceiling of his bedroom. God, he hated holidays. Wouldn't have taken this one, had his producer not insisted. And all because Tristan had almost collapsed three days ago when he'd returned from covering the military coup of another tumultuous Central American country.

Hell, who wouldn't have collapsed? He'd gone nearly seventy-two hours without a full night's sleep, had been pushed, shoved and shot at, spent an ungodly number of hours on a plane he'd bet would never get airborne, and had arrived home at two in the morning to be greeted by some burly military types for "debriefing."

This two-week rest really wasn't necessary, he thought resentfully, wondering what normal people did when they found themselves with an entire day on their hands and nothing to do to fill the hours.

The telephone rang. He might have welcomed the diversion if he didn't so clearly remember the call he'd received only the day before. He'd been twiddling his thumbs then, too and hadn't minded going off to Sara's rescue. Of course, he hadn't known that he would come home feeling twenty years older—and totally discouraged after having met a beautiful, very interesting woman.

Crossing his fingers in the hope that this wasn't Sara again, he cautiously pulled the receiver to his ear. "Yes?"

"I understand I owe you for coming to my daughter's rescue yesterday."

"Oh, hullo, Neal. Yes, you owe me," Tristan answered somewhat grimly. "I'll decide later what form of repayment I require."

Neal chuckled. "Was it a trying afternoon?"

"Doesn't she ever make *you* feel ninety years old?"

"Frequently," Neal assured him. "So, how's the vacation coming along?"

"Slowly. Very slowly."

Neal laughed again, knowing his friend's feelings about forced inactivity. "What? No beautiful companion to help you pass the time?"

"Alas, no." Tristan thought of Devon and scowled. "I understand you have a date tonight."

"Yeah. Sara's scheming, I'm afraid. You met Devon yesterday?"

"Yes. She's lovely."

"She is very attractive."

Neal didn't sound exactly ecstatic over his plans for the evening, Tristan noted with interest. "Don't you like her?"

"Sure, she seems very nice. But—"

Tristan sat up in bed. "But—?"

"Well, I'm really not in the market for marriage right now, you know? Sara's got this crazy idea that I'm going to be lonely and miserable after her wedding, and I can't convince her that I'm actually looking forward to being on my own for a while. Hell, I've never even lived alone. Went straight from my parents' house to a college dormitory room and then to single parenthood. I may just find I like being footloose for a change."

Though Tristan didn't want to argue with Neal, particularly just now, he doubted that his friend would enjoy living alone as much as he thought. Tristan had lived alone for so many years that he knew exactly what it was like. He also knew Neal wasn't the type to appreciate it. Neal was the classic family man—enjoyed having his loved ones around him, sharing his breakfast table. If it hadn't been for his single-minded dedication to raising Sara and making a success of his business, Neal would have been married years ago. Tristan suspected it wouldn't be long before his friend would be cohabitating again—maybe even with Devon Fleming.

Long after the brief telephone call was concluded, and Tristan had risen and dressed and eaten a hearty breakfast, he found himself still wondering why the thought of a relationship between Neal and Devon bothered him so much. He didn't even know the woman, after all; had met her only once, briefly; was no more interested than Neal professed to be in entering a long-term, serious relationship. Had he become so spoiled that he expected any woman he found attractive to fall at his feet? Was he so greedy that he wanted all the pretty ones for himself, begrudging even one to his best friend?

But the truth was he didn't begrudge the others to Neal; only this one. After only one short meeting, several long, shared glances and all-too-brief touches, Tristan wanted Devon Fleming for himself.

It wasn't as if Neal were particularly interested in Devon, he argued. Had Neal staked a claim, Tristan would have respected it. But Neal was obviously going out with Devon to please Sara more than himself. Which meant that maybe he wouldn't be too annoyed to find himself facing competition from his best friend. Because, despite his reluctance to alienate Neal in the process, Tristan hadn't given up hope of seeing Devon again. Soon. Without Sara—or anyone else—as a chaperon.

TRISTAN WAS DISAPPOINTED when a woman he'd never seen before answered Devon's door that afternoon. Standing on the doorstep with his hands in the pockets of his pleated gray slacks, still trying to come up with a logical explanation for being there, he frowned at the attractive Oriental woman who'd opened the door. "Is—uh—Devon here?"

"She's here, all right," the woman answered with a startling Southern accent and an impish smile. "I've got her in the back room modeling a wedding gown I just finished. She said she wasn't expecting anyone. Is there something I can do for you?"

Tristan smiled, wondering what the odds were that he'd find his way to that back room. "No, I'm here to see Devon. It's personal, not business."

The woman eyed him speculatively. "You're that TV reporter, aren't you? Tristan—"

"Parrish," he supplied. "May I come in?"

"Sure." She moved out of the doorway, allowing him to pass her into the living room. "I'm Mali. I work for Devon."

"Mali," he repeated, studying her dark-almond eyes and smooth gold-tinged skin. "That's a Thai name, isn't it?"

She nodded. "My mom's Thai. Daddy's an ex-G.I. from here in Atlanta. I was conceived in Thailand, born in Georgia."

Tristan chuckled, wondering if the woman was so friendly and open to every stranger. "You say Devon's in the back room?"

"Yes, but she's modeling a dress. She's exactly the same size as the woman we made it for and I couldn't wait to see it on someone, so I talked her into trying it on. It's the most detailed dress we've ever done and I have to confess that it's exquisite."

Tristan had always believed it was his overactive curiosity that had led him into reporting. He suddenly wanted very much to see how Devon Fleming looked in the "exquisite" wedding gown.

"Which room is she in?" he asked, heading for the hallway.

Mali stared at him for a moment in indecision, then shrugged and followed. "She's going to kill me," she commented without a great deal of concern.

"Possibly both of us," Tristan agreed.

"Possibly." Mali walked quickly down the hallway, giving Tristan little time to look around. The house was bigger than he'd thought; he'd guess there were four bedrooms and at least three baths. Most of the doors were closed. Mali led him to an open one at the end of the hallway. "Devon?"

"Who was it, Mali?" Devon's voice asked from inside the room. "Another fabric delivery? I'd almost forgotten we were expecting one this afternoon."

"It wasn't a delivery," Mali replied, grinning at Tristan over her shoulder.

"No? Then who was it?"

"A visitor for you."

Standing just out of Devon's sight, Tristan grinned at the overheard reaction. "Oh, damn. Get me out of this dress, will you, Mali? There's no way I can undo all these tiny buttons myself. Who is it, anyway?"

"I believe I'll announce myself," Tristan interjected when Mali would have answered. He stepped past her into the bedroom doorway, then stopped short at the sight of Devon, standing before a tall cheval mirror, her hands at her sides as she stared at him in shock.

The afternoon sun streamed through the white eyelet curtains of a window behind Devon, framing her in golden light. The dress was the purest white, glittering with seed pearls and what might have been tiny rhinestones sewn into the intricate lace covering the tightly fitted bodice and the long, full train. Smooth peach skin showed through the sheer fabric from the lace band collar to the low-cut décolletage. The sleeves puffed high at the shoulders, then hugged her slender arms, tapering to form lacy points at her wrists.

She'd pinned her honey-brown hair up, leaving her back exposed almost to the waist by a deep, plunging vee of sheer fabric that ended in a row of tiny pearl buttons leading to the ruffle topping the elegant train. Her waist looked impossibly tiny above the full skirt, which was appliquéd with more lace and shimmering stones.

Tristan had once been kicked right in the center of the chest by an angry revolutionary who'd studied martial arts. He remembered that feeling now as he looked at Devon. Breathing suddenly became an almost-impossible task.

"Tristan!" she gasped.

He knew she couldn't be half as stunned as he was. "I've never seen anything more beautiful in my life," he said simply.

She flushed pink and looked quickly down at the dress, her hands plucking nervously at the skirt. "Thank you," she murmured. "We're very proud of this dress. It's one of our nicest ones yet."

"I wasn't talking about the dress."

She looked quickly back up at him, her eyes widening, blush deepening. "Oh," she whispered.

"I think I'll be running along now," Mali said cheerfully. "I'll lock the door behind me. See you, Devon."

Tristan had forgotten the other woman's presence. He turned to tell her goodbye, but she was already gone. He heard the front door closing just as Devon came out of her dazed silence and called out, "Mali, wait!"

"Too quick," Devon complained. "I needed her to help me with these buttons."

Tristan took an eager step forward. "I'd be more than happy to offer my assistance."

"No!" She held up a hand, taking a step backward. "I'll manage, thank you. Why are you here, Tristan?"

For the life of him, he couldn't remember the semiplausible excuse he'd come up with for visiting her this afternoon. He glanced around the fabric- and pattern-cluttered room, fumbling in his mind, finally settling on a weak substitute. "I was afraid I'd offended you yesterday. I came by to offer an apology, if necessary."

She tilted her head inquiringly, drawing his attention back to her long, slender throat. He shoved his hands quickly into his pockets, his fists clenching. God, she was beautiful.

"You didn't offend me yesterday," she told him, obviously puzzled. "Why would you feel you owe me an apology?"

"Well, I did criticize your sketch. The one with the ruffle," he clarified quickly.

Her expression cleared. "But, Tristan, Sara explained that I wasn't particularly happy with the peplum on that dress. I only sketched it to show her how it would look. I was relieved when you helped me talk her out of it."

"Then no apology is necessary?"

"No, but thank you for your concern." She glanced back down at her borrowed finery and cleared her throat. "I really should change back into my clothes. Since we've gotten that settled, I won't keep you."

"Are you asking me to leave, Devon?"

She looked startled. "Of course not," she assured him quickly, as if worried that she'd offended him this time. "I only thought— Would you like to stay for a cup of coffee? Or tea, maybe?"

He smiled without a twinge of guilt about his deliberate manipulation. "Yes, I'd like that, thank you. I'll wait outside in the hallway until you've changed."

"I'll hurry," she promised, her hands already moving to the small of her back.

"I'm in no rush," he assured her quietly. It was with great reluctance that he stepped outside the room and closed the door behind him.

Only when he was alone in the hallway did he allow himself to release a long gust of air and slump dazedly against the wall. Had any woman ever affected him the way Devon had when he'd seen her in that gown? He would never have dreamed he'd have been aroused by a woman dressed in a virginal white wedding gown— in fact, he would have assumed the very sight of a wedding gown would cause him to break out in hives. But

Devon had been stunningly beautiful. Like a— Like a fairy princess. Or an angel. Straight out of a dream.

He blinked in astonishment at the fanciful direction his thoughts had taken. How very unlike him. Maybe his producer had been right, after all. Maybe Tristan *did* need a long rest. How else could he explain his unprecedented reaction to this woman?

He was still trying to analyze his response to her when he heard her make a sound of frustration, followed by what might have been the stamp of a small foot. After a long moment of silence, Tristan called out, "Devon? Is anything wrong?"

There was a brief pause before she answered. "It's these buttons," she said, her door-muffled voice exasperated. "They're so tiny. I can't—"

He smiled when her words trailed off. "Would you like some help?" he offered. "I promise I'll be a gentleman about it."

He thought he heard a muttered curse and his smile deepened at the thought of her standing embarrassed and annoyed in her lace and ruffles. And then the door opened behind him, slowly. "I need help," she said with a sigh. "And I'm going to strangle Mali the next time I see her for leaving me like this. She was the one who insisted I try on the dress."

"I don't blame her for wanting to see it on," Tristan replied. "She must have spent hours on this dress. Did she do the beading herself?"

"Mali and I both worked the beading—along with another of my employees, Betty. And you're right, we have many hours invested in it," Devon confirmed, standing stiffly while Tristan reached for the top button.

"Lord, these buttons are tiny, aren't they? I hope the bride will have someone to attend her when she dresses for the wedding."

"There are usually plenty of eager hands to help the bride dress."

"And an even more eager pair of hands to help her *un*dress," Tristan suggested.

"So I assume."

The dress parted beneath Tristan's helpful fingers, baring a length of silky spine. Suddenly aware that she wore nothing beneath the garment, he fought the need to clear his throat, sternly reminding himself that he'd promised to be a gentleman. Now, why had he done that?

When the last button opened, he couldn't resist the urge to run one fingertip down her back, from her nape to her waist. "I wonder if the bride will look half as lovely in this as you do."

"Better, I hope," Devon replied, her voice sounding strained. "After all, she's paying me to make her look beautiful."

He would dearly have loved to allow his lips to follow the same path his fingertip had taken. Instead, he forced himself to step back and steer the conversation into less intimate channels. "Just how much would a dress like this set one back?" he asked bluntly, curious as to what Devon would charge for her work. He hoped she wasn't selling her talent and expertise too cheaply.

The figure she named made him choke. "*That* much?" he asked in amazement. So that explained how she made the payments on this nice home and paid two assistants.

She winced and turned to him, one hand holding the loosened dress at her throat. "I know it sounds like a lot, but this is imported silk and alençon lace. And the pearls and rhinestones have all been hand sewn as well as the—"

He stopped her with a smile and an upraised hand. "Devon, it isn't necessary to justify your cost to me. I'm sure the lady will never regret a penny of the price of this gown. She'll treasure it for her lifetime."

Devon seemed pleased. "I hope so," she said. "I like to think perhaps her daughters will wear it—and maybe *their* daughters." She flushed a little and dropped her gaze. "I guess I'm overly sentimental."

"I think you're utterly delightful," Tristan replied quietly.

Devon's eyes rose slowly to his, and held for a long, silent, heart-stopping moment. Tristan felt himself going under fast. If he had any hope of honoring his promise to be a gentleman, he'd better get out of this room *now*. "I'll—uh—wait for you in the living room," he announced tightly, turning to leave before he had the chance to change his mind.

"Thank you for the assistance," she said as he stepped through the doorway.

His hand on the doorknob, he smiled back at her. "Believe me, it was my pleasure." And then he closed the door between them. Firmly.

ALONE IN THE ROOM, Devon sagged nervelessly, allowing the dress to slip off her shoulders and fall to her waist. She stepped out of it automatically, taking care not to crush it. Ideally, the garment should have been lifted over her head, but she certainly couldn't have asked Tristan to help her with *that*.

Tristan. What was he doing here? she asked herself for the dozenth time since he'd startled her with his arrival. And why had Mali suddenly bolted, as though her presence was clearly superfluous? Surely Mali hadn't thought there was anything going on between Devon and Tristan Parrish!

Utilizing the straps sewn into the garment to evenly distribute its weight, she arranged it on a padded hanger and hung it on a rack with two other, less elaborate gowns. All too conscious that Tristan was waiting for her, she dressed hurriedly in the lacy bra, white sweater and navy slacks she'd worn before trying on the gown. Facing the cheval mirror, she pulled pins out of her hair, allowing it to tumble softly to just below her shoulders. She ran her fingers through it in lieu of using a brush, slipped on her shoes, and she was ready. But still she hesitated before leaving the room, hoping another few minutes would help her control the slight tremor in her hands.

It would be a long time before she'd forget Tristan's expression when he'd first seen her in the gown. No man had ever looked at her quite that way before. He'd looked . . . stunned. Hungry. Almost primitive.

And then he'd flashed that oh-so-charming smile of his and her knees had weakened.

She didn't know why he was here. She didn't for a minute believe he'd come just to offer an apology for an imagined offense. But, whatever his reason, Devon had had few opportunities to spend time with a man like Tristan. Suddenly breaking into a smile, she realized she was wasting time hiding in a back room when a sexy, famous man was waiting in her living room. She checked her appearance one more time in the mirror, then hurried to join him.

He wasn't waiting in the living room. Frowning in bewilderment, she wondered if he'd left, and was aware of a sharp stab of disappointment. And then she heard a sound from the connected parlor, and she followed it curiously. She found Tristan leaning over the conference table, studying a thick album of photographs of the gowns she'd designed. He looked up when she entered.

"Devon," he said, smiling, "you're a genius. These gowns are incredible."

She flushed warmly in reaction to his praise, though she chided herself for doing so. Other people had complimented her on her work—why did Tristan's opinion matter so much? "Thank you," she responded. "This is what I love to do."

"Where did you study?"

"I have a degree in fine arts from the University of Georgia. My grandmother taught me to sew when I was ten. I helped put myself through college by working in the alterations department of an exclusive bridal store. Then a friend with a problem figure asked me to help design her wedding gown. That one was such a success that one of her bridesmaids, who was also engaged, asked me to do hers. And then someone brought me an antique size-six dress that she wanted altered to fit her size-ten body, without visible signs of the alteration. One thing led to another, and before long I had more business than I could handle part-time. That's when I went into business for myself."

"Very impressive," Tristan observed, looking back down at the book.

"People like the idea of having a gown that's unique," she explained. "I've never reproduced any design exactly. I may use many of the same features, particularly if the dress is for one of the boutique lines, but I always do something differently so that each dress is one-of-a-kind, whether a wedding gown, flower girl's dress or a formal gown for a high-school prom. I also give my clients a wide range of options in price, depending on how detailed the design or how expensive the materials we choose."

"Is it the lighting, or is this wedding gown pink?" he asked, peering intently at the page he'd just turned to.

She walked closer to stand beside him. "It's white lace over pink silk taffeta," she confirmed. "And the veil is a very pale pink net. Pastels have become popular for wedding dresses in the past couple of years. We did a lavender gown last spring—such a pale lavender it was almost white. It turned out beautifully. Peach is another favorite."

Tristan frowned and shook his head, turning to an elaborate, Scarlett O'Hara-style white gown. "Wedding gowns should be white," he proclaimed. "Whoever heard of a purple wedding dress?"

Devon chuckled. "Not everyone looks good in white," she reminded him. "Off-white—what we usually call 'candlelight' or ivory—has always been popular. Of course, most brides still choose white, even for second marriages. It's the color of celebration."

Tristan pointed to a photo of a striking redhead in a slinky black sequined minidress. "Don't tell me this was a wedding gown. Now, that really *would* be too avant-garde for my traditional tastes."

Laughing, she shook her head. "She wore that to accept an award. I told you, bridal gowns aren't all I do."

Tristan closed the album and reached for an open sketchbook nearby. "This is nice. A suit?"

She nodded, studying the sketch with some pride. The jacket was closely fitted, with long, clean lines and a low-cut neckline. The straight skirt fell to a flirty kick-pleat at the knees. She'd added a hat to the sketched figure, picturing it in tightly woven white straw with a white net band. "Liz Archer wants to be married in something sophisticated and elegant. I suggested a white moiré silk suit. She likes the idea."

"This looks just right for Liz. Cool and classy, with hints of smoldering sensuality."

Devon blinked at his assessment of her best friend's personality. He was right, of course. Was he that good at summing up all women? Or was he drawing on his years of acquaintance with Liz's brother? Liz had mentioned Tristan many times, but had always made it clear they'd never dated. She'd jokingly said that she had too much common sense to get involved with a charming daredevil with a penchant for adventure and variety.

Thinking of Liz reminded Devon of her upcoming date that evening with Neal. She bit the inside of her lip, wishing . . .

"Would you like some coffee?" she asked Tristan abruptly, trying to distract herself. "Or do you prefer tea?"

"Tea would be very nice, thank you," he answered. He smiled down at her, making her vividly conscious of how closely together they stood. She started to move away, only to stop short when he lifted a hand to brush a strand of hair away from her cheek. His fingers lingered, lightly stroking the line of her jaw. "Am I keeping you from your work?"

Her eyelids felt heavy in response to his sensual touch. She held them open with an effort. "No, I . . . have some spare time this afternoon."

"So do I." He smiled. "Would you mind very much if we spend that spare time together?"

Held mesmerized by his silvery blue eyes, Devon moistened her lips. "I'd like that," she said in little more than a whisper.

His smile faded as he dropped his gaze to her mouth. "So would I," he murmured. "Very much."

3

TRISTAN KNEW he had to leave, that he'd put his departure off as long as possible. They'd had their tea and slices of an excellent coffee cake she'd told him her grandmother had made for her. There was no reason for him to remain any longer. Except that he really didn't want to go.

Devon had proven to be every bit as delightful as he'd thought her during their first brief meeting. She was quick and funny and bright. He'd never felt as relaxed with any woman as he had during their afternoon tea. Nor had he ever had such a difficult time keeping his hands off a woman.

She sipped her tea, and he wanted to catch her in his arms and taste its drops on her lips. She bit into her cake and he trembled with a need to feel her nibble at his skin. He found himself wanting Devon as if he'd been celibate for years—as if he were a teenager alone for the first time with the girl of his dreams.

He didn't know exactly what it was she did to him. He only knew that he liked it.

He wanted very much to ask her out. It would be easy enough to invite her to dinner the following evening, he thought longingly. And yet—

It was utterly ridiculous, of course, that he felt so very guilty when he thought of Neal. It wasn't as if his friend had a claim on Devon, he reminded himself yet again. It wasn't as if Neal had even pursued her for their date. It had all been Sara's arrangement. Not Neal's, not Devon's. Yet still Tristan felt as if he were moving in on a friend's territory—something he'd never done in his otherwise-rather-feckless life.

He couldn't ask her out, he finally, reluctantly decided. Not until after her date with Neal. If it turned out that she and Neal hit it off—well, Tristan could step out of the picture. It wouldn't be easy—particularly if he found himself forced to socialize with Neal and Devon—but he could do it, for Neal's sake. And yet, if nothing came of tonight's arranged date— Well, Tristan was all ready to take over. At least now, Devon had become acquainted with him; an invitation from him wouldn't come as a total surprise to her.

He was doing the right thing, he told himself as Devon escorted him politely to the door. He'd made the right decision.

She held the door open and smiled up at him. "It was nice seeing you again, Tristan."

Tristan was almost as surprised as Devon when he reached out and caught her to him for a long kiss. He hadn't planned on it. And yet he couldn't bring himself to leave her without first letting both of them find out what it could be like between them.

Devon stiffened at first when his mouth covered hers. And then, to his utter delight, her lips softened and parted beneath his, her hand lifting to rest lightly against his chest. He muttered his approval, just managing to resist deepening the kiss. He certainly didn't want to spoil the moment by going too far too soon.

His entire body groaned in protest when he pulled away from her. Somehow he managed to smile. "I'll see you again," he promised.

Looking slightly dazed, she nodded. "Yes."

He touched her cheek one last, quick time before stepping outside and closing the door behind him. He didn't bother to don the jacket he held slung over one shoulder. He needed to cool down, he thought with a rueful glance at his indelicately tight slacks. He was still smiling when he crawled behind the wheel of his sports car. The smile held until he glanced at his watch and realized that Neal would be picking up Devon in a couple of hours.

He wondered with a scowl if Devon would go to sleep that night with Neal's kiss lingering on her lips, rather than his own. And he hoped very much that she'd be going to bed alone.

"SARA SEEMED DELIGHTED with the sketches of her gown. That was all she could talk about over dinner yesterday."

Devon smiled across the restaurant table at Neal. "I'm glad she liked it. I was rather pleased with the design myself."

"Good. I'd like her to have whatever she wants, of course. She'll only be getting married once—I hope," he added soberly.

Feeling the need to reassure him, Devon looked at him seriously. "Sara seems to be a very determined young woman," she said. "I think if she's set her mind to making a success of this marriage, she'll do it."

Neal nodded, looking rather pleased. "You may be right," he agreed. "She and I talked about the problems facing her—facing every young married couple—and she seems prepared for them. She's aware that divorce is the easy way out at times, but she and Phillip both say they intend to spend the rest of their lives together. If anyone can make a marriage work, it's probably Sara."

"I'm sure you're right." That subject exhausted, Devon picked up her tea glass and sipped slowly, trying to think of another topic of conversation. Neal wasn't hard to talk to, and he was certainly easy to look at. Tall, slender, tanned, fit. His eyes were dark blue, like his sister's; his smile easy and charming, like his daughter's. His hair was dark, but at forty, he was beginning to gray. Streaks of silver gleamed in the restaurant's subdued lighting, making him only more attractive. And yet every time she looked across the table, Devon found herself fighting the memory of Neal's blond, sexy best friend. Dammit, why couldn't she stop thinking of Tristan Parrish? She barely even knew the man!

And yet she couldn't stop thinking of the feel of his body pressed to hers, his mouth moving on hers. Couldn't stop remembering how easily they'd talked over tea and cake, in contrast to this rather stilted conversation with Neal. Couldn't help wondering what it would be like to be out with Tristan, to face him across a candlelit table—to have him go home with her afterward.

"Did you say something, Devon?" Neal asked politely, making her wonder if she'd groaned aloud.

"No."

"Oh." He cleared his throat and toyed with his dinner for a moment.

Devon took pity on him, deciding it was her turn to initiate a conversation. "I talked to Liz this morning. She's really very happy, isn't she?"

Neal smiled. "Yes. She and Chance make a good couple. He's a nice guy. A little rough around the edges, but he's crazy about Liz. They're much better suited than she and her first husband were."

"I'm designing her wedding suit. And Holly insists she's taking the wedding photos, whether Chance cooperates or not. It seems he hates posing for pictures."

Neal chuckled. "Apparently. But if anyone can get him to cooperate, it would be Holly."

Something about the way he said Holly's name made Devon look at him more closely. But he was smiling in much the same indulgent manner that he had when he'd talked about his daughter, so Devon decided she must have been imagining undercurrents that simply weren't there—probably because she knew Holly thought Neal was a "major hunk," in her bubbly younger friend's words. Holly had raved about Neal for an hour after meeting him the first time—the same day Devon had met him. Devon had asserted that Neal was much too mature and conventional to keep up with Holly, who'd merely shrugged and changed the subject.

Devon wondered what Holly would say when she met Tristan. *Speaking of "major hunks,"* she thought with a secret smile. And then she almost sighed in exasperation when she realized she'd drifted into thoughts of him again, though she'd promised herself she wouldn't during her date with Neal.

She was actually relieved when it was time for Neal to take her home. She couldn't help wondering whether she would have enjoyed the evening with Neal more had she not had the afternoon with Tristan to compare it with. A tiny voice inside her asked if it was possible Tristan had shown up at her house for that very reason. It seemed hard to believe that he could be that interested in her—and yet he'd kissed her. And what a kiss it had been!

She wondered if it was terribly foolish of her to long for Tristan to kiss her like that again—and soon.

"TRISTAN, OLD CHAP, it is my impression that you are snockered," the overly bright-eyed, somewhat flushed cameraman pronounced gravely, peering owlishly across the bar table. "And not a terribly jolly drunk, at that."

Sprawled in a comfortable barrel-backed chair across from his co-worker, Tristan scowled. "I hate it when you attempt a British accent," he grumbled, his own accent pronounced. "We do *not* find it amusing."

Mitchell Drisco chuckled and downed the remainder of the beer from his fifth—or was it sixth?—mug.

Tristan couldn't remember exactly how many drinks they'd had since meeting at this popular watering hole for reporters and off-duty cops. He couldn't exactly say he was having a good time. But at least it gave him something to do rather than sit around his house and wonder how Neal and Devon were getting along on their date.

"Hell, Parrish, no one does snooty royalty better than you," a burly black man in a rumpled patrol uniform commented, one massive arm propped on the table as he lingered over his first and only drink of the evening. Hal wasn't much of a drinker, but he enjoyed winding down with the others at the bar. He and Tristan had known each other for several years, and were as friendly as two men could be who had absolutely nothing in common except a wry sense of humor and a dedication to their respective jobs.

The fourth occupant of the table-scaled-for-two was a woman. Her long legs stretched out, booted feet crossed on an empty chair in front of her, she sprawled in her seat, looking oddly graceful despite her slouched posture. Her chin-length sable hair was mussed, whatever makeup she'd applied that morning faded, her sweater and wool slacks wrinkled from a long day's work, but still she drew assessing approval from the bar's male patrons—present company excluded. Tristan, Hal and Mitchell had known Tyler Jessica Harris long enough to accept that she was much more interested in an exclusive story and a front-page byline than she was in romance.

"Our friend seems to be in a royal snit tonight," she remarked perceptively, studying Tristan over the rim of her beer mug. "What's wrong, Tris? Do you hate being on vacation this badly, or is it something else? Woman problems, maybe?"

Mitchell snorted. "Woman problems? Parrish? Sure, T.J. Now tell us another story."

Tristan's scowl deepened. "Just becaush—er—because I've had a bit more to drink than usual does not mean I'm having problems—woman or otherwise."

"So who is she?" T.J. asked interestedly, ignoring his denial. "Don't tell me there's one woman in Atlanta who can resist your Continental charm?"

Tristan muttered a curse into the dregs of his fifth— or sixth—beer.

Hal cocked his head curiously. "It *is* a woman, isn't it, Parrish? What's the prob? She married?"

"She's not married," Tristan muttered. "And there *is* no woman," he added quickly.

"She's not married," T.J. repeated. "So what is it? Does she hate men?"

Tristan sighed. "She doesn't hate men."

"She hates you?" Mitchell suggested with a grin.

"She doesn't hate me. Can't you people find something else to talk about?"

"When a woman has our cool, unflappable heart-throb friend moping into his beer? No way," T.J. replied.

Tristan narrowed his eyes at her. "Whatever made me once think I actually liked you?" he countered. "You're a heartless snoop, Tyler Jessica."

"Of course. I'm a reporter," she answered, unperturbed. "And if you ever call me Jessica again, you're going to walk funny for days. Got that, Parrish?"

He only grunted and finished his beer.

"So how come you're not pursuing the elusive lady instead of hanging out with us losers?" Mitchell inquired, propping both elbows on the table as he looked across at Tristan.

"Speak for yourself, boy," Hal mumbled around a mouthful of popcorn. "I'm no loser. Just got lousy taste in drinking companions."

"It's a good question, though," T.J. pointed out. "Why *are* you here, Tristan? Where's the lady this evening?"

"Out with my best friend," Tristan explained glumly. He looked around and snapped his fingers at a bored, weary-looking cocktail waitress. Or, rather, he tried to snap his fingers. They didn't seem to be cooperating. "How about another beer?" he called out. She nodded and waved at him to wait his turn.

He turned back to the table to find his companions staring at him. "What?" he demanded.

"You're after your best friend's woman?" Hal asked. "That's low, man."

"Even for you," Mitchell added with a disapproving shake of his head.

Stung, Tristan sat up straighter. "She is *not* his woman! They hardly know each other. It's their first date."

Mitchell nodded gravely. "Oh. So he beat you to the punch, eh?"

"You could say that."

"And this is how you react?" T.J. motioned expressively toward the two empty beer mugs sitting in front of him.

"I'm being noble," he informed her curtly. "I'm staying out of the way until he has his chance with her. If he blows it, that's his problem."

T.J. curled her lip. "What typical male arrogance. *You* are giving *him* his chance with her. Doesn't she have anything to say about it? What if she happens to prefer him? Or you? Or what if she wouldn't have either of you served on a silver platter?"

Tristan shifted uncomfortably in his chair. He wasn't accustomed to being accused of sexism. He had a reputation of being a totally modern male, though no one had gone so far as to call him sensitive. Still, he realized that he had been thinking in terms of possession and conquest with Devon. What was it about her that brought out his more primitive instincts?

"She's right, you know," Mitchell announced solemnly. "You should leave it to the lady to decide. But first you ought to let her know you're interested. How's she going to choose you if she doesn't even know you're in the running?"

T.J. sighed. "It's not a beauty pageant, Mitchell. You make it sound as though she's going to name a winner and a first runner-up."

Mitchell grinned unrepentantly. "Maybe Tristan will get Mr. Congeniality."

Tristan muttered something derogatory about Mitchell's ancestry—a slur that was met with no more than a laugh.

"Much as I hate to admit it, Mitch may have a point," Hal said. "Maybe your lady doesn't know you're even interested, Tristan."

Tristan thought of the kiss. *Damn, what a kiss!* "I think she knows," he murmured.

"Then it's up to her now, right?" T.J asked logically.

Tristan nodded. "Yes. It's up to her now."

He wondered if his friends would be totally disgusted with him if they knew that he was hoping Devon and Neal were having a really terrible time on their date. "So, where's that beer?" he complained, looking around again for the waitress.

SEATED AT HER vanity table, dressed in the soft, warm nightgown her mother had given her for Christmas, Devon pulled a brush through her hair and thought back over her date. She supposed it had been successful. After a few awkward false starts, she and Neal had talked easily enough. He'd brought her home after dinner and left her at the doorstep with a smile and a seemingly sincere assurance that he'd had a very nice time. He hadn't kissed her good-night. Nor had he asked her out again. She had to admit she was relieved that he hadn't done either.

It had been a very nice date with a very nice man. And it had left her restless and yearning for something . . . something more. More exciting. More intense. More adventurous. More blond, blue-eyed and British.

Devon groaned and hid her face in her hands, cursing herself for wanting what she knew could only be bad for her in the long run—like chocolates and caffeine and a sexy reporter named Tristan Parrish.

The sound of her doorbell brought her head up sharply. A quick glance at her bedside clock told her it was nearly midnight—two hours after Neal had brought her home. She really didn't think it was Neal. So who—?

The bell rang again. And held. She jumped to her feet and snatched up her quilted satin robe, pulling it on as she hurried into the living room. Thoughts of tragedies and accidents filled her mind, bringing her heart into her throat. Surely a visit this late could only be bad news. Half expecting to see a policeman's uniform, she looked out the small window in her front door.

"What the—?" She snapped on the porch light and jerked the door open. "Tristan! You scared me half to death! What are you doing here at this hour?"

He frowned as though giving her question his full attention. She studied him in bewilderment, noting his overbright eyes, rather flushed cheeks and rumpled hair and clothing. Surely he wasn't—

"I—uh—don't remember why I'm here," he admitted finally, giving her a sheepish smile.

Oh, mercy. He was. "You're drunk!" she accused in exasperation.

He nodded. "Yes. I'm sorry."

Sighing, she reached out and took his arm. "Honestly, Tristan. Is it really necessary to act out the stereotype of the hard-drinking reporter? Come in and I'll make coffee."

"I don't usually drink excessively," he explained carefully, obediently following her urging. She noted with suppressed amusement that he walked even more elegantly in this condition than he usually did. But very slowly.

She led him to the couch and helped him out of his brown leather bomber jacket. "Then why did you drink so much tonight?"

"I'm on holiday," he replied, as if that should explain everything.

"This is your idea of a good time?"

He sighed deeply. "No. I don't want to be on holiday. I hate not working. But just because I was a bit overtired after my last assignment, the producers thought I needed a rest."

"Why do you hate vacations? Most people enjoy taking time off from work."

"Most people have something to do when they're not working," he replied with an overemphasized shrug. "I don't."

"No hobbies? No favorite pastimes?"

"No. Just work."

She watched as he leaned his head against the back of the couch, sprawling bonelessly across the pastel floral cushions. "No wonder you and Neal are such good friends," she commented, remembering what Liz and Sara had told her about Neal. "You're both compulsive workaholics."

Her mention of Neal's name made Tristan frown and lift his head to look at her. "You went out with him tonight."

She lifted one eyebrow. "Yes."

"How was it?"

The blunt question made her blink. "It was very nice. I think I'd better make that coffee now."

"Did he ask you out again?"

The touch of belligerence in his voice brought her chin up. "That's really none of your business, is it?"

He looked as though he wanted to make a hasty retort. Instead, he groaned softly and dropped his head back against the cushions. "I suppose not. Sorry."

"I'll make the coffee. Why don't you close your eyes and rest?"

His eyelids drifted shut. "An excellent idea."

She studied him for another moment, utterly bewildered, then shook her head and walked toward the kitchen. She couldn't imagine what Tristan Parrish was doing on her couch at midnight, decidedly intoxicated. They hardly knew each other! Why hadn't he gone to someone he knew for assistance if he hadn't wanted to be alone?

The coffeemaker had already been prepared for morning, so all she had to do was turn it on. While the coffee brewed, she decided to check on her unexpected caller again. She wasn't particularly surprised when she found him sound asleep, half lying on the couch, his cheek against a mint-green throw pillow. The rather feminine upholstery made him look all the more masculine in contrast—sleek and tanned and strong. Her stomach muscles contracted sharply.

Her hand wasn't quite steady when she reached out to touch his shoulder. "Tristan?"

His eyes half opened. "Mmm?"

"You didn't drive yourself here, did you?"

He frowned without raising his head. "I—uh—" And then he seemed to remember. "No. I came in a cab. I wonder why I gave this address?" he asked meditatively.

"Would you like me to call a cab to take you home?"

"Yes, thank you. But first I'd like to rest a moment, please." And he closed his eyes again.

She couldn't help smiling. He was being so terribly polite. How could anyone maintain such dignity while lying half on, half off a couch?

She was probably going to regret this, she thought as she reached down to slip off one of his tan suede shoes. The sensible thing to do would be to call a cab and send him home. She tugged off his other shoe and dropped it beside the first. And then she grasped his ankles and lifted his legs to the couch. He squirmed into a more comfortable position without opening his eyes. Still smiling faintly, she fetched a soft hand-knitted afghan and draped it over him.

His eyes opened when she tucked the afghan around his shoulders. She went still, trapped in the gleaming silver-blue of his eyes. "Devon," he murmured.

She swallowed. "Yes?"

"D'you have another date with Neal?"

The man had a one-track mind. She sighed imperceptibly and gave in. "No, Tristan."

His sensual mouth curved into a satisfied smile. "Then will you go out with me?"

She bit her lip against an answering smile. "Maybe," she prevaricated. *If you remember asking me, that is,* she added silently.

He seemed to accept that as a definite. His eyelashes drifting closed again, he muttered something that sounded like, "He had his chance." And then he fell asleep.

Thoroughly bemused, Devon knelt beside him for another long moment, studying his face. He was just as attractive in sleep as he was awake, she decided, unable to repress images of him lying in her bed, sharing her pillow. She couldn't resist reaching out to brush a strand of gold-tipped hair away from his forehead. Something told her he was going to be terribly embarrassed in the morning. She really should have sent him home. But she realized she wasn't at all sorry she hadn't.

"Good night, Tristan," she whispered.

She never would have imagined she'd go right to sleep with a man she hardly knew sleeping on her sofa only a room away. Surprisingly enough, she did. And she was still smiling when she drifted off.

4

TRISTAN WAS AWARE of the dull headache before he was even fully awake. Without opening his eyes, he frowned, trying to remember exactly what he'd done the night before. He recalled downing one beer after another, moping so pathetically into his drinks that his friends had teased him. Whatever had gotten into him? He'd never been a sloppy drunk and had no intention of starting now.

He shifted his weight. His arm fell over an edge and dangled to the floor. His frown deepened. The floor shouldn't be so close to his bed. Had he . . . ?

He opened his eyes, then closed them again with a groan, knowing exactly where he was. And the things he'd said after arriving. Why couldn't he be one of those lucky fellows who mercifully forgot their foolish drunken behavior, rather than recalling it in mortifyingly clear detail?

Never again, he thought forcefully. *I'll never drink beer again. Or anything else, for that matter.*

"Good morning." Devon's voice had a distinct undertone of amusement. She'd obviously noted his chagrin at waking up to find himself on her sofa.

Resigned to the inevitable, he opened his eyes again to find her standing a few feet away, looking fresh and lovely in a peach sweater and winter-white slacks, her hair soft and loose to her shoulders. If she was annoyed or disgusted by his behavior of the night before, it certainly didn't show in her amused brown eyes.

"Good morning." He shifted cautiously upright, pushing aside the afghan she must have covered him with. His head thudded in protest at the movement, but he ignored his discomfort, too intent on repairing the damage he'd so stupidly done to his chances of getting to know Devon Fleming—closely. He ran a hand through his disheveled hair and grimaced ruefully. "It appears I owe you an apology."

She crossed her arms comfortably at her waist and watched him with a smile. "Do you?"

"Yes. Please believe that I don't usually behave this way—getting drunk and showing up on other people's doorsteps, I mean. My only excuse is that I was thinking of you last evening and I must have given your address to the cabbie."

Devon cocked her head, apparently intrigued. "You were thinking of me? Why?"

Since he'd been so successful at sitting upright, Tristan decided to attempt standing. Very slowly he rose to his feet. Only then did he smile at Devon. "After the kiss we shared yesterday, do you really have to ask why I couldn't get you out of my mind?"

She looked both pleased and endearingly flustered. "Oh." She glanced down at her hands, which were suddenly twisting at her waist, then shyly back up at him. "Are you hungry? I'll make breakfast."

He wanted very much to agree, not for the food, but for the excuse to linger awhile longer with Devon. Deeply ingrained manners forced him to voice a protest. "You really shouldn't go to all that trouble. After all, it's not as if you invited me to stay the night."

Her smile returned, to his pleasure. "True," she conceded. "But since you're here, I might as well feed you. Do you like blueberry waffles?"

"More than life itself," he assured her gravely.

She laughed and it was all he could do not to pull her into his arms and kiss her. Had any woman ever looked more desirable to him?

"The bathroom's down the hall and to the left if you'd like to freshen up," she told him. "Breakfast should be ready in twenty minutes."

"Thanks." He watched her turn and head for the kitchen. He stopped her just as she was about to leave the room. "Devon?"

She looked over her shoulder. "Yes?"

"I really am sorry about last night."

"Consider yourself forgiven," she answered lightly and then disappeared before he could say anything else.

Smiling to himself, Tristan found his shoes and put them on before going in search of the bathroom. His head still hurt, but a hangover was a small price to pay for breakfast with Devon Fleming.

"AFTER THE KISS WE SHARED yesterday, do you really have to ask why I couldn't get you out of my mind?" Sliding the hot waffle onto a plate, Devon replayed Tristan's words in her head, for at least the dozenth time since

he'd spoken them. Had their kiss really affected him as deeply as it had her? Or was that only a practiced line, intended to weaken her resistance to him?

And then she almost snorted at her own thoughts. Resistance? *What* resistance? She hadn't attempted to resist Tristan Parrish since he'd first smiled at her.

Was the blazing attraction truly mutual? Or was he one of those men who had to make a conquest of every woman he met? Who couldn't let even his best friend go unchallenged when a woman was involved. After all, Tristan had seemed quite concerned about her date with Neal. Why?

Frowning at her thoughts, she checked the maple syrup warming in the microwave. It really didn't matter why he was here, did it? Tristan *was* attracted to her. He was probably quite accustomed to this sort of thing, though Devon had rarely been the recipient of attention from a man like this. Men like Tristan were usually more attracted to Brandy. Devon would be an idiot not to enjoy the attention while she had it; after all, she mused, what if she never had a chance like this again? She simply had to keep in mind that men like Tristan weren't interested in long-term relationships.

Other women enjoyed brief, amusing affairs without ending up heartbroken. Why shouldn't she have a little fun before settling down for life with a "nice" man—like Neal Archer, for example?

"Nasty weather out, isn't it?" Tristan commented, joining her in the kitchen.

Surprised by his words, Devon looked out the window over her sink, noticing for the first time that it was raining—a gray, cold-looking, uninviting rain. "Yes, it is."

Tristan looked around her warm, bright kitchen with a smile of approval. "It's so much more pleasant in here. Those waffles smell heavenly. I hadn't even realized I was hungry until I came in."

"I thought we'd eat in here, rather than the dining room. There's fresh orange juice on the table. Would you like coffee?"

"Yes, please." He headed for the coffeemaker.

Devon stopped him with an upraised hand. "Sit down. I'll get it."

She set a well-filled plate in front of him, then poured coffee for both of them. "Did you leave your car somewhere last night?"

He shook his head. "I took a cab to the bar, on the off chance that I shouldn't be driving home."

She looked up from the waffle she'd just sliced into. "So, you did intend to get drunk last night?"

"No, of course not. It just—" He broke off with a grimace, then quickly changed the subject. "These waffles are delicious."

Devon smiled. "I'm glad you like them."

"Tell me about yourself, Devon."

She reached for her orange juice. "What would you like to know?" *And why?*

"Have you always lived in Atlanta?"

"I grew up in rural Georgia, about forty miles from here. My mother and grandmother still live there."

"Do you have any brothers or sisters?"

"A younger sister. Brandy."

"How much younger?"

"Four years. She's twenty-four."

"Are you close to your family?"

She wondered if she imagined a note of wistfulness in his question. "I'm close to my mother and my grandmother."

"And your sister?"

She hesitated. "Brandy and I are very different," she answered finally. "She's a bit of a rebel, likes to be outrageous and spontaneous."

He cocked his head in interest. "And what is Devon like?"

The question made her self-conscious. How was she supposed to respond? "I've asked myself that question a few times lately," she said finally, trying for levity.

Tristan seemed to find her answer quite revealing. "You fascinate me, Devon Fleming."

She flushed and concentrated on her food. "Finish your breakfast before it gets cold," she ordered.

Tristan chuckled, but complied.

TRISTAN HELPED DEVON clear away the breakfast dishes, then remarked with obvious reluctance that he really should be going. He looked at the heavy rain still pelting against the window and scowled.

"Do you have plans for the day?" Devon asked, remembering his complaint that he hated vacations because he didn't know what to do with himself when he wasn't working. She found it awfully hard to believe there weren't several attractive women he could call to help keep him entertained, but he'd apparently been on his own the night before, as he seemed to be now. Why didn't this beautiful, larger-than-life man have a woman in his life?

Tristan shook his head, glancing down at his sleep-wrinkled clothing with obvious distaste. "No. I suppose I'll spend the day at home."

Brandy, of course would never send a man like this away without at least trying to entice him to stay, Devon thought wistfully. But then Brandy would know what sort of enticements to use. Whereas, all Devon could offer was . . . "Since I'd heard that it was supposed to rain all day, I rented a couple of movies to watch this afternoon. They're supposed to be quite good, though you may already have seen them. I know it's not a very exciting day, but . . ."

"Devon," Tristan broke in gently, "are you inviting me to spend the day with you?"

Her fingers twisted even more tightly at her waist. "If—if you'd like to," she said tentatively, cursing the shyness that had plagued her all her life.

Tristan's smile made her pulse flutter wildly. "I'd like that," he replied. "Very much."

Swallowing the sudden lump in her throat, Devon hoped she hadn't just made a very big mistake.

Tristan glanced down again at his rumpled clothing. "I'd enjoy this much more if I didn't feel quite so grubby. Would you mind terribly if I popped over to my place to change first?"

Devon was so intrigued by his deep, British-sounding voice that she hardly noticed what he'd asked. "I love your accent," she said without thinking. "How long have you lived in the States?"

"Nearly sixteen years—since I was twenty-two," he replied, brushing at a particularly noticeable wrinkle in his once-crisp slacks.

"Did you move here with your family?"

He ran a hand over his beard-shadowed chin and scowled, though she wasn't sure whether his displeasure wasn't directed more at his dishevelment than at her questioning. "No," he said finally. "I came over alone. My mother's American, so I have dual citizenship."

Devon reminded herself that he'd asked questions about her family, though he didn't seem particularly eager to talk about his own. "Do you see your family often?"

"I went back five years ago—to attend my father's funeral," he answered flatly, his hands going into his pockets.

"Oh. I'm sorry."

He shook his head. "We weren't close. Would you mind if I use your telephone to call a cab?"

The conversation about his family was obviously at an end. "There's no need to call a cab. I can drop you off and then you can drive back in your own car after you've changed."

"Thank you, but that's not necessary. I'd hate for you to have to go out in this miserable weather."

"I wouldn't mind," she assured him with a smile. "Really."

Tristan reached out to touch one hand lightly to her cheek. "You're a very nice person, Devon Fleming."

Nice. Not exactly a synonym for *exciting.* Or *sexy.* Or *wildly desirable.* Suppressing a sigh, she smiled and answered lightly, "Thank you. Are you ready to go?"

"Almost," he replied, lifting his other hand to cup her face between his warm palms. "But first . . ."

His mouth covered hers.

Tristan proved then, without doubt, that their first kiss hadn't been just a fluke. This one was just as exciting. Just as sexy. And made her feel just as wildly desirable. She was trembling like a leaf when it finally ended. Even more incredibly, Tristan's hands were no steadier than her own.

"Now I'm ready to go," Tristan said huskily.

Devon just hoped she'd remember how to start the car.

DEVON DROPPED TRISTAN off at his home—his very expensive, very impressive home in one of the best neighborhoods, she noted from the driveway—but politely refused an invitation to accompany him inside. She was both curious and surprised that he owned a house rather than a condo, but she wasn't quite ready to enter his home. "I'll wait for you at my place," she told him. "I have a couple of calls to make."

"Then I'll see you in an hour," he promised, reaching for the door handle.

"Do you like fried chicken?" she asked impulsively.

"Yes."

"I'll pick some up on the way home. We'll have that for lunch."

He shook his head. "You got the films, I'll provide the lunch. See you in an hour, Devon. Drive carefully."

And then he was gone, dashing through the pouring rain, his jacket collar turned up against the chill. Devon watched him until he'd disappeared from sight. Only then did she sigh dreamily, shift into Drive, and pull away from the curb.

TRUE TO HIS WORD, Tristan rang her doorbell only an hour after she'd dropped him off at his place. Her heart tripping, Devon took a deep, steadying breath and opened the door. His hair gleamed gold, looking stylish in the layered cut he favored. When he passed her on the way inside, she noted that he smelled of soap and a faint, citrusy after-shave. He'd changed into a black bomber jacket, pleated black slacks and a beautifully cut charcoal-gray shirt. He looked wonderful. But then, she'd thought he'd looked just as good earlier, heavy eyed, unshaven and sleep tousled.

"I've arranged for our lunch to be delivered at one o'clock," he informed her, slipping out of his jacket. "That should give us time to watch one of the films, shouldn't it?"

Delivered? He must have ordered pizza, Devon decided. "Yes, that's plenty of time," she assured him. "Make yourself comfortable, Tristan. Could I get you a drink? I have cola or fruit juice—or I think I have a couple of cans of beer, if you'd rather have that."

Tristan grimaced comically. "No beer. I've sworn off the stuff after last night. Cola's fine."

She laughed. "I'll be right back."

He was sprawled comfortably on the couch when she returned with two tall glasses of iced cola. He patted the cushion beside him. "I saved you a seat."

She cleared her throat soundlessly and nodded as she set the glasses on the table in front of the couch. "I'll just put the movie in the VCR first."

When she could stall no longer, she walked slowly to the couch. She perched stiffly on the opposite end from Tristan, a good three feet of cushion between them, all too aware that he hadn't stopped watching her since he'd arrived.

Tristan grinned and reached out to haul her closer, one arm snugly around her shoulders. "You told me to make myself comfortable, didn't you?" he reminded her when she looked up at him in surprise. "Isn't this much more comfortable?"

Devon forced herself not to stiffen. "Yes, I suppose it is," she agreed weakly, pressing the Play button on the remote control.

Tristan chuckled and reached for his soft drink, keeping Devon close while he settled more deeply into the cushions to watch the movie. So conscious of his nearness, she took a while to relax and concentrate on the film. Gradually, it began to seem more natural to sit so close to Tristan, hearing his quiet laughter in her ear, exchanging amused comments about the clever dialogue and slapstick antics on the screen.

The rain drummed steadily against the windows and heavy clouds darkened the skies outside so that the living room was illuminated only by the flickering television and the small lamp at Tristan's elbow. The resulting cozy intimacy made Devon feel warmly content. Yet beneath the quiet pleasure was a physical awareness that was more exciting than anything she'd felt in a very long time—if ever. She never would have dreamed that sitting quietly on a couch, watching a movie, could be so intensely arousing.

The film ended on a satisfying note and Devon pushed the Rewind button. "I enjoyed that, didn't you?" she asked.

Tristan's arm tightened around her. "Very much," he said, turning her face to his with fingertips pressed to her cheek. "The movie wasn't bad, either," he added just before he kissed her.

The remote control fell unnoticed to the carpet. Devon wound her arms around Tristan's neck and kissed him just the way she'd been wanting to kiss him from almost the first moment she'd seen him.

Their mouths seemed made to fit together. Tristan's covered hers so perfectly, so skillfully. The tip of his tongue touched her lower lip, then slid warmly into her mouth. She opened willingly to him, eager to taste him. Lost in the kiss, she was only dimly aware of his hand stroking her back through the soft peach sweater. She arched into his touch and tangled her tongue with his.

Tristan groaned deep in his throat, pulling her even more closely against him, so that her breasts were crushed erotically into his chest. Devon buried her fingers in his luxurious hair, pulling her mouth from his to draw a breath before pressing a kiss to the sexy dimple at the corner of his mouth. He'd wrapped her hair around his right hand, holding her in position for his kisses, which he scattered hotly, heedlessly, over her face and throat.

"Devon," he muttered hoarsely. "Devon, I—"

The doorbell chimed suddenly, cutting off whatever he might have said. Tristan grimaced. "That will be our lunch."

Still dazed by their kisses, Devon blinked and tried desperately to clear her mind. "What?"

He laughed shakily and set her gently away. "I'll get it. You wait here a moment."

Devon's hands felt icy against her burning cheeks when she covered her face in astonishment at her own behavior. Had she really just climbed all over a man she'd known for only forty-eight hours? That wasn't at all the sort of behavior befitting a "terminally good" girl!

She lowered her hands and smiled thoughtfully before rising to follow Tristan into the dining room. Only to stop short in amazement. "Tristan! What—?"

Thoughts of pizza and fast-food fried chicken abruptly left her mind. Two rather damp, white-coated waiters, one tall and dark, the other shorter and sandy-haired, bustled around her dining room, setting the table with a white linen cloth, china and silverware. Roses and candles graced the center of the table as the waiters pulled more and more items from a seemingly bottomless container.

Tristan smiled at the look on Devon's face and stood behind a chair, waiting to seat her. "I hope you're hungry."

She would not cry, she told herself sternly, slowly taking her chair and allowing Tristan to slide it forward. He probably did this sort of thing all the time. He'd think she was an idiot to be so incredibly moved. It was just that no one had ever done anything like this for her.

With friendly efficiency the waiters served the meal—Cornish hen, buttered pasta laced with caviar, steamed asparagus in herbed butter, golden scones resting beside pats of butter. Devon intended to eat every bite. She couldn't help wondering how he'd arranged all this in the short time he'd been away from her.

The dark-haired waiter hovered at her elbow, a glistening bottle in hand. "Champagne?"

She managed a smile. "Yes, thank you."

He returned the smile and poured Dom Pérignon champagne into a crystal flute.

"We'll serve the rest ourselves," Tristan said, slipping something into the waiters' hands. "Thank you. And tell Claude I owe him one."

"Sure. We'll return for the dishes in—say, two hours?" the sandy-haired waiter suggested.

"That will be fine."

When they were alone, Tristan took his seat, draped his snowy napkin across his lap and smiled at Devon. "I hope Cornish hen is a satisfactory substitute for fried chicken."

Her answer came out as a sniffle and an infuriating trickle of tears.

"If **you** had your heart set on fried chicken, I'd be happy to make a run to the Colonel's," he offered.

She gave a watery giggle and wiped her eyes with a corner of her napkin. "Don't be ridiculous. This is the sweetest thing anyone has ever done for me." And she'd had to go and mess it up by getting sappy, dammit.

His face softening with his smile, Tristan reached out to pull her hand to his lips. "I wanted to thank you for being so kind to me last night. You probably should have kicked me out on my ear for imposing on you in that disgusting condition."

She couldn't help smiling in return. "You weren't disgusting," she assured him. "Actually, you were quite elegant—very dignified."

He winced and shook his head in self-disgust. "I can't imagine what came over me." He kissed her hand again before releasing it. "We should eat before the food gets cold. Save some room for dessert. I ordered chocolate ganache cake with raspberries—it's a specialty at my friend Claude's restaurant."

Devon sighed happily. "It sounds heavenly."

Tristan assured her that it was.

She couldn't remember ever having a more romantic meal, nor a more charming companion. She couldn't imagine any woman ever being able to resist this man. She had no intention of even trying.

She wanted to enjoy every minute of Tristan's attention—even if it lasted no longer than one enchanted, rainy day.

5

BOTH DEVON AND TRISTAN would probably have been hard-pressed to describe the movie they played that afternoon after lingering a long time over lunch. They were only a third of the way into the film when the waiters returned to competently clear away the remains of lunch, but Devon hadn't been able to fully concentrate on the movie even before that interruption.

They were sitting close again—his arm around her, her head nestled into the hollow of his shoulder, her bare feet drawn up beside her. Tristan had kicked off his own shoes and stretched his legs out comfortably in front of him. No man had ever looked sexier to Devon.

Tristan stroked the backs of his fingers against her cheek. "You have the softest skin," he murmured. "And so very fair."

"I can't tan," she admitted. "I burn very easily."

His free hand came around to touch her jaw, turning her face up to him. "It would be a crime to harm this skin," he observed, his gaze caressing her face.

At the moment her fair complexion was proving very inconvenient. She felt heat flooding her cheeks at his touch, at his nearness, and knew she was blushing deeply. Yet all she could do was stare up at him, longing for something she didn't quite have the courage to name, even to herself.

His lips touched hers lightly, fleetingly. Her eyelids grew heavy, though she managed to keep her eyes open. Tristan touched his mouth to her forehead, and then her cheek. "So soft," he breathed. "So sweet."

She raised a hand to his chest, resting it unsteadily against his heart. She was delighted to feel it pounding heavily.

Her own pulse raced recklessly. She turned her head in search of his mouth, wanting more than those fleeting kisses.

He gave her all she could have asked for—and more. This kiss rocked her all the way down to her bare toes.

Tristan didn't content himself with exploring her mouth, though he did that quite thoroughly. His hands roamed her back, down her arms, finally slipping under the hem of her sweater to stroke the skin beneath. His palm was so warm, so excitingly rough. She would have expected Tristan's hands to be smooth, but they felt strong and callused. Deliciously so.

No one had ever kissed her as hungrily, as completely, as Tristan did. Every kiss she'd known in the past faded to insignificance in contrast. Had those few other men been so inept with their caresses? Or had they failed to satisfy her simply because they hadn't been Tristan?

She slid her hands up his arms to his shoulders, discovering that his elegant physique was misleading. Surprisingly firm, work-hardened muscles rippled beneath her hungry hands. She wondered what he did to stay in such admirable shape.

He slanted his mouth to a new angle and kissed her again. She parted her lips and enticed his tongue back into her mouth, her own welcoming it eagerly. When he slid his right hand between them to cup her left breast, she didn't even attempt to demur. Instead, she arched into his touch, her nipple peaking against the lace of her wispy bra, straining for a more intimate exploration.

Tristan dragged his mouth from hers and groaned her name. And then his lips were on her throat, his fingers kneading the fullness of her swollen breast. Devon gasped and allowed her head to fall back, her eyes closed, her fingers clenching in his hair.

She wanted him. She'd known him only two days, expected nothing more from him than a few fleeting moments of pleasure, but she wanted him as she'd never wanted anyone before.

Tristan shifted his weight, bearing her down into the couch behind her. He lay draped half across her, pressing their bodies into the floral cushions. Groping for the remote control, he pressed the Stop button, then tossed it aside.

"Devon." Tristan whispered her name in her ear before nipping lightly at her lobe. She quivered in response. "Ah, Devon, you're so lovely. So special."

"Tristan." She spoke his name experimentally, loving the sound, the feel of it. He slid lower against her, lifting her sweater to expose her stomach to his seeking mouth. Her breath caught in her throat. "Oh, Tristan."

His slender hips moved against her leg. She felt his arousal pulsing through his slacks. Her thighs tightened as warmth flooded her. Her skin felt hot, her breathing was almost painful. An empty ache centered in her being, waiting for him to assuage it.

He pushed her sweater higher and smoothly unclasped the front of her bra. Devon shivered as cool air brushed her exposed breasts, though she wasn't cold. Quite the opposite, in fact. And then Tristan's mouth was on her breast, his tongue curling around the hardened nipple. She gasped and pressed against him.

Tristan turned his attention to her other breast, using his lips, tongue and teeth to drive her to trembling incoherence. Wanting to explore more of him, she slipped one hand inside the loose collar of his shirt, to stroke his neck with her fingertips. He lifted his head to look down at her, his bright eyes making her think of blue fire, his golden hair tousled around his beautiful face. Holding her gaze with his own, he reached deliberately for the top button of his shirt, released it, then paused as though to give her a chance to stop him.

Stop him? Oh, no. In only a few magical hours, Tristan had released the sensual side of her that she'd suppressed for so very long. She reveled in that freedom even as she wondered at her own uncharacteristically wanton behavior. Moving his hands aside, she unfastened the next button herself.

Tristan smiled his approval, waiting only until his shirt was unbuttoned before shrugging out of it and tossing it aside. Her sweater and bra followed. Lost in admiration of him, Devon forgot to be self-conscious of her own seminudity.

He was such a beautiful man. Lean, strong, firm, lightly tanned. Golden hairs curled riotously on his chest, almost hiding an assortment of scars she suspected were the result of his enthusiastic pursuit of his career. She pushed the thought aside, knowing that if she dwelled for long on his job and reputation, her own insecurities would resurface to spoil her pleasure in this moment. She traced a fingertip from the hollow of his throat to circle one brown nipple and then trail slowly down his flat stomach to the fastening of his black trousers. Tristan drew in a sharp breath.

"I want you, Devon," he said, his voice rather hoarse. "I can't quite remember ever wanting anyone this badly."

She didn't believe that for a minute, of course. But it was such a nice thing to hear that she smiled. "I want you, too, Tristan." She could have told him that she'd never wanted another man as much as she wanted him, and it would have been absolutely true. She knew better than to make herself that vulnerable to him.

Tristan kissed her lingeringly, crushing her breasts against his chest, then raised his head again, his expression darkening with regret. "Maybe I'd better go."

"*Go?*" Devon repeated in dismay, staring up at him. "But why?"

His smile wasn't steady. "I find myself short of willpower when I'm with you. If I stay, I'm going to have to make love to you."

Devon slid a hand behind his head. "Do I look as though I'm trying to stop you?" she demanded.

He caught her hand in his own, pulling it around to press a kiss to her palm. "You've only known me for two days. As much as I want you, I'd understand if you prefer to wait until you know me better."

She liked the implication that they'd be seeing more of each other. But she didn't need any more time to realize she wanted to make love with Tristan. She'd known from the beginning that he was the man who could show her everything she'd missed in the few bland, vaguely unsatisfactory relationships of her past. She wanted so badly to discover what Tristan could teach her about passion. About her own sensuality.

She drew the tip of one finger lightly across his lower lip, noting the muscle that suddenly twitched in his jaw, hearing his breath catch. "Are you telling me that you'd like to wait?"

He groaned. "The first time I saw you I wanted to throw you over my shoulder and carry you to the nearest bed."

"Tristan, I'm surprised. That seems so primitive, coming from you."

His eyes narrowed at her teasing tone. He leaned over her, crushing her into the cushions. "You make me feel very primitive, Devon Fleming. I've been clinging to civilized behavior by my fingernails all day. Haven't you noticed?"

She smiled as she thought of the elegant luncheon, the snowy linens and delicate crystal. "You've done an admirable job of it."

He circled her slender throat with one large hand. "You wouldn't mock me, would you, love?"

She told herself that the endearment meant nothing, that it was a word Tristan would toss out easily. "Of course not, Tristan," she assured him with exaggerated sincerity.

He laughed softly and pressed a kiss to her smiling lips. "I want you." And suddenly he wasn't laughing. "If you want me to go . . . If you'll have any regrets . . . Tell me now," he said urgently. "I'm not sure I can bear it if you change your mind later."

Her arms went around him, bringing her body flush to his. "No regrets," she promised huskily. "This is what I want."

He buried his face in her hair. "I hope so, Devon. I truly hope you're right."

Devon squirmed out from beneath him, stood and held out her hand to him. "I'm in the process of remodeling my bedroom, but if you don't mind a bit of a mess . . ."

He rose and took her hand. "I don't mind at all."

DEVON'S ROOM smelled of fresh paint. She'd taken down the lace curtains and hadn't yet replaced them; bare miniblinds provided privacy in the meantime. Just enough light penetrated the blinds to show that the walls had been stripped of the old paper. Rolls of new paper in a contemporary design were stacked on the floor beside a large, unopened bucket of paste and a pile of wallpapering tools.

Devon bit her lip as they entered, but Tristan didn't seem to mind—or even to notice—the clutter. He had eyes only for Devon. Standing beside her bed, which was made up with sheets and a handmade quilt in lieu of the new bedspread stored in another room, he turned to take her in his arms. She forgot all about the unfinished decor when he lowered his mouth to hers.

Rising on tiptoe to lock her arms around his neck, Devon pressed closer, loving the erotic tickle of his chest hair against her breasts. His hands slid slowly down her back to cup her buttocks and lift her more snugly against him. His hips flexed slowly, and she felt his hardness against her abdomen. She ached for more.

His mouth never leaving hers, he laid her on the bed, her hair fanned out beneath her. His hand fumbled at her waist. And then he stood and swept her slacks away, stepping out of his own before returning to her, boldly, unselfconsciously aroused. Devon welcomed him back into her arms with a blissful sigh.

"Are you on the Pill, love?"

She stiffened at his question. "No," she replied with consternation. "It's been so— There hasn't been any—"

She stopped in frustration, aware that her words hardly conveyed the image of the modern, sophisticated woman she'd attempted to project.

Tristan smiled and stroked her cheek reassuringly. "Would you forgive me if I admitted I brought something with me—just in case?"

"I would be extremely grateful," she answered fervently. She wasn't sure she'd have survived stopping, now that they'd come this far.

As Devon had eagerly expected, Tristan did, indeed, show her everything she'd been missing. Passion. Fire. Intimate laughter. Raw, raging hunger. Any inhibitions she may have brought to her bed swiftly vanished beneath his skillful, avid hands.

Arching, writhing, gasping, Devon abandoned herself to his guidance, secure in the knowledge that he knew exactly what he was doing, where he was leading them. By the time he plunged into her, he was shaking as powerfully as she. She was pleased to note that his movements had grown more frantic, less polished; more impetuous, less deliberate. Together they rode to the edge of madness, and together they cried out when they tumbled helplessly into it.

Stunned, Devon lay beneath Tristan as they recovered, his face buried in her throat, his damp body shuddering with his ragged breathing. She'd known it would be different with him, she thought in bemusement. But how could she have known it would be like *that?*

She stroked his back with one unsteady hand, feeling the pulse still racing beneath his skin. Was it always like this for him? Did he always give himself so totally, so generously?

But, no. She wouldn't think of things like that. She'd let nothing destroy the enchantment of her time with Tristan. No regrets. No comparisons. No secret longings. If this was all she would have, it was well worth the risks.

She was fully aware that there was much more to her feelings for Tristan than mere sexual attraction—dangerously more. But she chose, for now, to push those feelings aside. If she didn't acknowledge them, they couldn't hurt her. She hoped.

TRISTAN FINALLY FOUND the strength to lift his head, though his limbs still felt astonishingly rubbery. Belatedly realizing that he was still lying on Devon, he shifted with an apologetic murmur to relieve her of his weight. Even then, he wasn't able to release her, and drew her into his arms to hold her cradled against his side.

Devon. What a delight she was! He knew full well that she'd acted entirely out of character with him, that she wasn't a woman who would ordinarily make love on such short acquaintance. He hoped her response to him indicated that she had been as deeply, as immediately affected by their meeting as he.

Though Tristan had been with his share of women—perhaps more than his share, were he to be completely honest—no one had ever made him feel like Devon did. Lovemaking had never driven him quite so high, moved him so much.

Everything was different with Devon. He couldn't quite analyze the difference, didn't even want to try at the moment. He simply wanted to enjoy her.

Smiling in the paint-scented, deeply shadowed room, he snuggled her closer and listened contentedly to the sound of the rain against the window. They had plenty of time yet to define their relationship, he told himself drowsily, his eyes closing as he rested his cheek against her soft, tumbled hair. They might even have the rest of their lives.

DEVON WOKE WITH A START at the chime of her doorbell. Disoriented, she pushed her hair out of her eyes and shoved herself up on one elbow, looking over Tristan to the clock radio on the nightstand beyond him. Six o'clock . . . in the evening she realized, noting the darkened room. She and Tristan had been sleeping for over an hour.

The doorbell rang a second time. Devon reached for her robe, wondering who it could be. Tristan stirred, then sat up. "Devon?" he murmured, his voice still thick with sleep.

She smiled at him. "Someone's at the door."

His own smile was drowsy, infinitely sexy. "Come back to bed and we'll pretend you're not home."

"Tempting," she admitted. "But I can't. It might be important."

He sighed and swung his long legs over the edge of the bed. "I could use something to drink."

"I'll get rid of whoever's at the door and then make us a snack," Devon offered. "I have more of Grammie's coffee cake. Meet me in the kitchen in fifteen minutes, okay?"

He grinned. "It's a date."

Making a hasty attempt to smooth her hair, Devon hurried down the hall toward the front door just as the bell chimed a third time. "Who is it?" she called out in habit from years of living alone.

"It's Holly. I brought your jacket back."

Tightening her robe around her, Devon swallowed a groan. Normally she would have welcomed this impromptu visit. But why had Holly had to come by tonight?

Devon opened the door to her petite, green-eyed, copperhaired friend, finding Holly damp and wind-blown and holding out a clear-plastic-covered sequined jacket she'd borrowed for a party the week before. "Since there's a strange car in your driveway, I know you have company and I won't stay, but I wanted to return this before—"

Her words faded to silence as she suddenly seemed to notice Devon's appearance. Devon managed not to grimace, though she knew full well she looked as though she'd just climbed out of bed.

Holly swallowed visibly and shoved the jacket into Devon's hands. "Oh, Devon, I'm sorry. I really came at a bad time, didn't I? But who would've thought—uh—I'll just go now, okay?"

Shifting the jacket into her left hand, Devon reached out with her right and grabbed Holly's wrist. "Don't be silly, Holly. Come in." She tugged her friend inside and closed the front door against the damp, chill evening air.

"I really have to go." Holly couldn't seem to quite meet Devon's eyes. In fact, Devon thought in bewilderment, Holly looked almost—devastated.

"Holly?" she asked in quick concern. "Are you all right? What's wrong?"

Holly shook her damp red head and shoved at her rain-spotted glasses. "I'm fine, Dev, really. So...I guess your date with Neal turned out pretty well, after all?"

Devon suddenly comprehended. So, Holly thought Devon had been in bed with Neal. An understandable mistake, since Holly knew Devon had been to dinner with Neal the night before. But Devon was startled at the extent of Holly's dismay. She knew Holly had been quite taken with Neal Archer the one and only time she'd met him; but had Neal really made this great an impression on her impulsive younger friend? And then, remembering how deeply Tristan had affected her from the moment he'd first smiled at her, Devon realized that it wasn't such a farfetched notion, after all.

"Holly—" she began, only to be interrupted by Tristan's voice behind her.

"Devon, where do you keep the tea? I've looked in the kitchen larder and I can't find it."

Devon looked over her shoulder to find Tristan standing in the doorway. He'd dressed in his slacks and shirt, though he hadn't tucked the shirt in. He wore his socks, but no shoes, and his thick blond hair was boyishly disarrayed. He looked magnificent, she thought with a suppressed sigh of feminine longing. "It's in the cabinet over the microwave, Tristan."

And then she remembered Holly. She turned her head to find her friend staring openmouthed at Tristan. A moment later, Holly looked back at Devon and smiled in delight. "Well, well," she murmured. "And just who is *this?*"

Amused at Holly's transparent relief, Devon almost forgot to be embarrassed. "*This* is Tristan Parrish," she replied. "Tristan, I'd like you to meet my very good friend, Holly Baldwin."

Tristan searched Devon's face quickly, rather uncertainly, as if wondering if he owed her an apology for his untimely appearance, but he seemed to relax when she smiled brightly at him. He took a few more steps into the room. "It's very nice to meet you, Holly. You're the photographer, aren't you? The one who's going to shoot Sara's wedding? Sara's told me all about you."

"Oh, you're *that* Tristan Parrish!" Holly said with a chuckle. "The TV reporter. I should have recognized you immediately. I've seen your work, and Sara talks about you all the time."

Tristan laughed. "Sara talks about everything all the time," he acknowledged. "To be quite frank, Sara *talks* all the time. But she's a love, isn't she?"

"She's a sweetie," Holly agreed.

Tristan gestured toward the doorway behind him. "Devon and I were just going to have some tea and cake. Would you join us?"

"Yes, do, Holly," Devon seconded immediately.

Holly shook her head. "Thanks, but I have to run. I just wanted to get that jacket back to you before something happened to it. Thanks again for letting me borrow it, Dev."

"Anytime."

"I'll get the tea started," Tristan said tactfully. "I'm sure we'll meet again, Holly."

"Oh, I love the way he talks," Holly breathed the minute Tristan had left them. "Particularly the way he says my name. Very Continental. And he's so gorgeous!"

"Mmm," Devon agreed, pleased to note that Holly's admiration of Tristan seemed purely platonic.

"So how about having lunch with me next week?" Holly suggested brightly. "I'm dying to find out how you managed to have dinner with Neal Archer and ended up in bed with his best friend."

Now Devon was embarrassed. "Holly!"

Holly laughed, winked at Devon and dashed out of the house before Devon could say anything more. Shaking her head in exasperation, Devon snapped the lock.

"Devon, I'm sorry," Tristan said the moment she joined him in the kitchen. His expression was sober. "When I heard the front door close, I thought you'd sent away whoever rang the bell. If I'd known your friend had come in, I wouldn't have just barged in like that. I hope you weren't too dreadfully embarrassed."

"Don't worry about it, Tristan. It was no problem. Truly." And it wasn't, Devon realized abruptly. She really wasn't all that perturbed that Holly had caught her with this fascinating man. As a matter of fact, she rather liked it.

Tristan didn't look entirely reassured. "Still, I—"

"Really, Tristan," Devon interrupted in amusement. "I'm a grown woman. No big deal, right?"

Tristan frowned as if something in her answer bothered him, but he let the subject drop. Instead, he fussed over their tea until Devon giggled at his finickiness.

"This," he told her loftily, sliding a delicate china cup in front of her, "is a perfect cup of tea. I can assure you you've never had one quite like it before."

Devon smiled and took a slow, cautious sip.

"Well?" Tristan demanded when she didn't immediately say anything.

"Perfect," she told him.

He sighed gustily and made a show of wiping his brow with the back of one hand. Devon giggled at his antics. And then gasped in pleasure when he caught her in his arms to kiss her half-senseless.

Neither of them particularly hungry after their big lunch, they decided to have sandwiches before their cake and call that dinner. Their conversation over the makeshift meal was hardly notable for its depth; in fact, Devon couldn't remember laughing so much in a very long time.

"Do you have plans for tomorrow?" Tristan asked when he'd finished the last bite of his cake.

"Very exciting ones," Devon answered dryly. "I'm papering my bedroom."

He looked surprised. "You're doing it yourself?"

"Yes. I'm as much a perfectionist with wallpaper as you are with tea," she teased. "If I do it myself, I feel as though I have more control over it."

"Dare I offer to help?"

She eyed him doubtfully. "Hanging wallpaper really isn't a great deal of fun, Tristan. Are you sure there isn't something else you'd rather do?"

"I can think of nothing I'd rather do than spend another afternoon with you," Tristan replied. "Unless, of course, you're growing tired of having me around. In which case you should say so."

Tired of him? She was more likely to grow tired of breathing. She tried to keep her answer light. "I'd love to have your help with my wallpaper, Tristan."

She thought his eyes had grown suddenly watchful, his words carefully chosen. "Then there's really no need for me to go home tonight if I'm only going to be back in the morning, is there?"

"You're welcome to stay the night," Devon said. "But you aren't exactly dressed for wallpapering. It's a very messy job."

He smiled faintly. "As it happens, I always carry jeans and a pullover in the boot of my car. In my job, I never know when I'll need to change into something sturdy."

"Then it seems you're well prepared," Devon remarked matter-of-factly. Did he really carry spare clothing as a requirement of his job? Or had he expected to spend the night with her again?

"I like to think so," he agreed.

She stood and stacked the few dishes they'd used into the dishwasher, sensing that he was watching her every move. "What would you like to do for the remainder of the evening?" she asked, straightening and turning to him.

He grinned devilishly and caught her in his arms. "Guess," he murmured, just before his mouth covered hers.

Wrapping her arms around his neck and pressing her body close to his, Devon found she didn't have to try very hard to guess what he had in mind. She had no complaints. There was nothing she'd rather do than make love again with Tristan.

6

"I'M TELLING YOU, TRISTAN, you didn't put enough paste
on the top right corner of this strip," Devon said,
smoothing the bottom of the wallpaper and looking up
at him as he balanced on a short ladder above her,
pressing the top half of the strip to the wall.

"I'm sure I used enough."

"Not on that corner," she insisted, standing to move
back and look up at it. The protective plastic covering
her carpet crinkled beneath her white leather sneakers
when she moved.

Tristan sighed and grimaced down at her. "You really are persnickety about your wallpaper, aren't you?"

She smiled. "I did warn you."

"So you did." He smoothed the paper one last time
with the plastic tool made for that purpose, then leaped
gracefully off the ladder and stood looking up at his
handiwork, hands on his hips, a smug smile on his face.

"Tristan, I really think—"

"Devon, trust me. It's fine. That paper isn't coming
down."

"Well, if you're sure," she said doubtfully.

"I'm positive," he declared, just before the top right
corner released its tenuous hold on the wall and fell to
drape sloppily over his head.

Devon propped her fists on her jeaned hips and sighed gustily, swallowing the laughter that threatened as a string of blue-tinged curses issued from beneath the paper. "What did I tell you?"

"*Don't* start on me," Tristan warned in mock anger, lifting the paper away. "Just be quiet and hand me the paste bucket."

Biting her lower lip against an enormous smile, Devon shook her head, causing her loose ponytail to bob gaily, and reached for the gallon-size plastic bucket.

She never would have dreamed she could have such a delightful time hanging wallpaper. It amazed her even more that Tristan Parrish could seem to be enjoying the mundane task.

Devon thought it was very likely that she'd enjoy doing anything, as long as Tristan was with her. He was funny, charming and sexy. More exciting than any man she'd ever known. Whether they were talking about his fascinating work or her designs, exchanging nonsense, or sitting quietly, he seemed perfectly content to be with her—which to her was a very flattering impression. And when he made love to her, as he had more than once during the night, he made her feel like the most beautiful, most desirable woman in the world.

So what if he did treat every woman in his life that way? she asked herself bravely. She was the one who had him now, and she intended to savor every moment.

"You're holding that strip upside down," she pointed out.

Tristan groaned, his blue eyes glinting with his smile. "Nag, nag, nag," he muttered, obediently reversing the paper. "Can you reach that brush, love?"

Every time he called her that, her knees threatened to melt. So much for remaining objective, she thought in exasperation, passing him the requested brush.

"Your bedroom's going to look very nice when you're finished," Tristan commented, admiring the sophisticated blue-and-gray floral-stripe wallpaper.

"Thank you. I was really getting tired of the old rosebud-and-lace look. It reminded me too much of my grandmother's room," Devon admitted. "This is more modern, I think."

He traced a stylized flower with one fingertip. "Very sensuous. Cool and classy and feminine. Like you."

She smiled in pleasure. "Thank you."

And then Tristan frowned. "Just whom are you intending to impress with your new bedroom decor?" he inquired.

"Myself," she replied pertly. "Be careful around that corner, Tristan. You'll tear the paper."

"Anyone ever tell you you're a tough taskmaster, Ms. Fleming?"

She grinned. "Now you see why no one else volunteered to help me hang my paper?"

"Yes, I believe I am beginning to understand. Are you like this with your employees when they're making up your designs?"

"I'm afraid I've been known to be," she admitted. "Fortunately my employees know that it's only because I'm so anxious for the dresses to turn out right so the customers will be pleased."

"A real Simon Legree, eh?" He stretched to wipe a smear of paste from a far corner of the paper.

Devon almost sighed aloud as she watched the muscle ripple beneath the ice-blue knit pullover that molded faithfully to his arms and torso and exactly matched his eyes. His jeans hugged his slender hips almost as closely as she had during the night. And though she'd believed the long hours of intense loving had left her thoroughly sated, she found herself growing warm and damp again, just remembering. And anticipating.

"Well, damn," Tristan grumbled when the sponge he'd been using slipped from his hand to plop onto the plastic below him.

Devon looked up from measuring the next strip and giggled. "You really are a klutz, aren't you, Tristan?"

He scowled repressively at her as he retrieved the sponge. "And *you* must like living dangerously. I warn you, my sweet, you'll pay for all your mockery."

She lifted an eyebrow. "I'm shaking in my tennies," she assured him gravely.

"And so you should be."

She really liked this man, Devon thought, going back to work with a secret smile. She refused to dwell on how easily "like" could turn to "love"—and happiness to heartache.

HIS ARMS CROSSED OVER his chest, Tristan leaned against the bedroom doorjamb and watched as Devon climbed the ladder to inspect the final strip of wallpaper. His approving gaze lingered on the slight curve of her hips through her snug-fitting jeans. He could almost feel those soft, satiny hips in his hands, as he had so often the night before. But not often enough, he mused, aware of the stirring in his groin. He was beginning to believe he could never have enough of this woman.

He raised his gaze slowly to her face. She was flushed and disheveled, her ponytail straggled on her neck, and the little makeup she'd applied that morning had faded away. There was a spot of dried paste on her cheek and her lips were pursed into a slight grimace as she peered closely at a seam. He'd never thought any woman more beautiful, nor had he ever wanted any woman more.

His unprecedented feelings for Devon were beginning to seem natural to him. He was comfortable with her. He felt no need to impress her, no reason to pretend to be anything he wasn't. She treated him like a man, not like a TV news star, or a "catch." She'd teased him over breakfast about the embarrassing nickname he'd been given during his Gulf War coverage the year before—to his eternal chagrin, the personality-hungry media had dubbed him "the desert dish"—but she seemed to genuinely admire his work, discounting the sometimes-embarrassing celebrity that accompanied it. He liked that.

He was even beginning to wonder if she could perhaps understand about the fiasco he'd made of his life in England, and the idiotic, rebellious behavior that had gotten him all but disowned by his family, who'd done everything but carry him onto a boat headed for the

States and out of their lives. He never talked about those years, had shared them with no one but Neal, who understood completely, having experienced a similar rift with his own demanding, snobbish family.

That common bond had formed a friendship between the two men that had lasted since they'd first met eleven years ago. Sara had been only nine, then; and Neal, a single parent making his name in the business world. Two years younger than Neal, Tristan had been a new reporter for a prominent Atlanta newspaper. He and Neal had met through their jobs, but their friendship had been immediate and personal. It had lasted through their various career clashes and changes, and their sporadic liaisons with women when they allowed themselves time from their single-minded pursuit of success in their respective fields. And yet this was the first time in all those years that Tristan and Neal had been involved in even the hint of a competition for the same woman.

Pushing aside vague feelings of guilt, Tristan determined to give Neal a call the very next day. He'd ask his friend to lunch. He wanted his relationship with Devon brought out in the open, and he wanted Neal to know that his feelings for Devon were strong and very, very serious. Perhaps that would make his actions easier for Neal to understand.

"Well?" he prodded, when Devon had inspected the wallpaper in silence for several long moments. "Is it perfect enough to suit you, lady boss?"

She tossed a laughing glance over her shoulder, making him ache to taste her smile. "Not perfect, but very close."

"I'm so glad you're satisfied. Now, will you please agree to a break for food? I'm wasting away for lack of sustenance."

She rolled her eyes and started down the ladder, still looking at him. "Honestly, Tristan, you just had all that pizza two hours ago for lunch. How could you possibly be—"

"Devon, watch the—"

But it was too late. Before Tristan could reach her in his abrupt surge forward, Devon stepped off the ladder—and straight into the bucket of thick, unused wallpaper paste. Both of them watched in dismay as her foot disappeared beneath the surface of the paste, her sneaker completely submerged, the bottom of her pant leg coated with the viscous mess.

"Oh, no!" Devon wailed, making an effort to free herself. The paste slurped noisily, holding her foot in its gooey grip. "Tristan, help! My foot is stuck. Oh, and it's so slimy and disgusting. Yuck!"

He tried not to laugh. He really did. For all of thirty seconds. And then he lost it.

"Tristan!"

He couldn't help it. Holding his ribs, he put back his head and howled.

"Well, thanks very damned much!" she huffed, setting him off again.

"*Now* who's the klutz?" he asked unsteadily.

She glared at him. "I'm supposed to think this is funny?"

He snickered. "It is from over here. If you could only see yourself . . ." And he laughed again.

Devon struggled to hold on to her frown . . . and then looked down at herself, standing with one foot up to the ankle in the paste bucket. And then she was laughing, too, clinging to Tristan's arm for support.

"You cad," she grumbled when she could talk again. "How dare you stand there laughing at me when I'm in peril?"

"I couldn't help myself. I just seemed to come unglued," he told her, earning a hearty groan from Devon for the bad pun. "Sorry, love. A true hero would have come to your rescue without a chuckle, wouldn't he?"

She sighed. "Well, you did warn me that I'd pay for taunting you," she pointed out resignedly. "And you didn't even have to arrange it. I stepped into this one all by myself."

He grinned. "You certainly did."

"If I humbly apologize for teasing you, will you please help me out of this bucket?"

"I'd be delighted," he told her, reaching down to cup her leg behind her knee and pull gently.

Her foot made a wet, glooping sound as it popped out of the slime, sending them both into the giggles again. And then Devon screwed up her face and looked in disgust at her paste-covered shoe and jeans. "What a mess."

"Wait, don't put your foot down yet. You'll get wallpaper paste all over everything."

She looked at him in question. "I'm supposed to stand here on one leg until it dries?"

"I have a better idea." Without giving her a chance to agree, he swung her into his arms, careful to keep her gooey foot away from him.

Devon clutched his shoulders for support as he headed for the bathroom. "What are you doing?"

He wondered if she weighed over a hundred pounds. She was so delicate, so fragilely made. A woman like this made a man feel very protective, even when he was teasing her, he mused contentedly.

"Tristan?" Devon repeated. "What—?"

He dumped her unceremoniously in the bathtub, steadying her until she had both feet firmly beneath her.

"Good idea," she approved. "I can stick my foot under the faucet and rinse the shoe off before trying to remove it. Much neater."

Without answering, Tristan kicked off his shoes and stepped fully clothed into the tub with her, pulled the curtain closed behind him and turned on the shower full blast. Devon gasped comically as warm water streamed over both of them, soaking them instantly. "Tristan! What in the—?"

"Well, we were both a bit grubby," he pointed out. "I thought a shower was in order."

She looked at him as though he'd lost his mind. "But we still have all our clothes on!"

He reached for the hem of her pink knit top. "Not for long," he announced, sweeping the sodden garment over her head and dropping it carelessly into the tub behind him.

Devon pulled her lower lip between her teeth in immediate comprehension. He was pleased to note that she wasn't protesting. Her eyelids grew heavy, the way they had the night before when he'd loved her. The shower had made her wispy brassiere go transparent and he could see her rosy nipples clearly through the lace. They hardened even as he watched. How he loved her responsiveness to him!

Neither of them was laughing now. Tristan cupped one full breast in his hand, his thumb circling her nipple as he teased at her lips. "Tell me you want me, Devon," he ordered huskily, needing suddenly to hear her confirm what he wanted so much to believe.

"I want you, Tristan. Oh, I want you so much!" she breathed, sliding her hands beneath his wet shirt.

He helped her rid him of the garment, then disposed of her bra. Now as eager as he, Devon removed her now clean shoes by shoving them off toe-to-heel and dumping them out on the bathroom floor. Hungrily Tristan hauled her against him, quivering when her wet skin brushed his and her breasts flattened against his chest. He crushed her mouth beneath his, pressing his hips urgently against her.

Breathing erratically, Devon reached between them and cupped him through his jeans, stroking the swelling length of him until he groaned and shuddered with the force of his need. And when she unzipped him and slipped her small, cool hand inside his briefs to grasp him more intimately, he ground out her name and lifted her against the tile wall behind her, his fingers digging into her still-clothed hips as his tongue surged deeply into her mouth.

For long, heated minutes they kissed and writhed together, their bodies arching in the timeless rhythm of lovemaking. When they were both desperate for more, Tristan slid to his knees, unfastening her jeans and pulling them and her panties slowly down her long, silky legs. And then his mouth was on her stomach, his tongue darting into the shallow indention of her navel.

Devon threaded her fingers into his hair, bracing herself against the tile wall with her legs spread. Which gave Tristan perfect access to the treasure between them. Holding her hips between his hands, he nuzzled into the wet honey-brown curls covering her delicate mound, loving the way her breath caught in response to his intimate caress.

"Tristan," she moaned, and then trembled when he touched her with his tongue. "Oh, Tristan. That feels so—*oh*—"

He was in no hurry now. Instead, he chose to savor the feel of the warm water cascading over his head and back, the sweet taste of Devon on his lips, the broken little sounds she made when he loved her. He could happily spend the rest of his life right here with her, he thought, deepening the caress until she cried out and clenched her fingers in his hair.

But it was inevitable that Tristan's urgency would grow. Devon's breath was catching in broken sobs by the time he surged upward to wrap her in his arms. Her arms closed around his neck and he flattened her against the wall, unable to get close enough to suit him.

He wanted to be inside her now, buried so deeply that he'd feel a part of her, and she of him. Impatient of his wet jeans still separating them, he shoved them far enough out of the way. And then he lifted Devon into his arms and plunged smoothly into her.

Devon gasped and wrapped her legs tightly around his hips, her arms tightening around his neck to steady her against him. He was dimly aware that he wasn't being gentle with her, but he was too far gone for restraint. Again and again he thrust himself into her; again and again she matched his movements driven by a greedy hunger of her own.

Tristan tried desperately to hold back his climax until he had brought Devon to her own, but then she wriggled sinuously against him and he was capable of doing nothing more than groaning her name and pumping himself into her as shudder after shudder of release ripped through him. Devon stiffened in his arms, her slender body bowing between him and the wall, and then she cried out as her own convulsions began. By the time they ended, it was all either of them could do to remain upright. The water was beginning to cool. Calling on their last reserves of energy, they quickly soaped and shampooed, then turned off the water and climbed out of the tub. Leaving a soggy pile of clothing behind them, they fell into Devon's bed and reached for each other again, as ravenous as they'd been each time before.

No, Tristan thought with one last glimmer of coherence, sinking blissfully into her, he'd never get enough of her. Never.

"Devon," he murmured, just before he covered her mouth with his.

TRISTAN COULDN'T HAVE said how much time passed before he stirred and frowned. "Devon?"

Drowsily she snuggled more deeply into his shoulder. "Mmm?"

"I'm not sure how to mention this—"

"What is it, Tristan?"

"I just realized that in the shower— Well, I'm afraid I got carried away. I didn't protect you, love."

She stiffened, then raised her head. "No. We didn't think about that then, did we?"

He tried and failed to read her expression. "Is this a bad time of the month for you?"

She thought a moment, then shook her head. "Actually, it's the very safest time for me," she assured him. "The chances are slim that anything happened."

"I'll be more careful from now on. I promise you that." He didn't want Devon to worry about any unforeseen consequences of their lovemaking. He'd never in his adult life been so irresponsible; he'd make sure he never was again.

"We'll both be more careful," Devon concurred. "Actually, I should do something about that myself. It shouldn't have to be up to you to remember every time. I'm a responsible adult. I should start seeing to my own needs."

Something in her voice made Tristan frown. He knew that it had been a while since she'd been involved with anyone, knew that Devon wouldn't give herself easily, regardless of how quickly she'd become involved with him. Yet she was beginning to sound as though she planned to make some changes in her way of life. Changing her bedroom, considering birth control. He could only hope that he was the motivation behind at least one of those changes. Tristan couldn't even think of her seeing another man—not now that he'd been with her.

He'd never been a possessive man before, any more than he'd ever been irresponsible in his relationships with women. Devon was changing him. He wasn't sure how, but something was different inside him. Something important.

He stared at the ceiling of her bedroom, dazed to realize that he was actually wondering how Devon would look carrying his child. And even more stunned that he wasn't breaking into a cold sweat at the very idea; in fact he found the idea very intriguing.

Yes, something was most definitely changing. He only hoped those changes wouldn't ultimately tear him apart after he'd protected himself for so very long.

THEY DECIDED TO GO OUT for dinner, since they'd spent so much of the weekend indoors. Devon plaited her hair into a neat French braid and wore a fresh sweater and slacks. Tristan donned the same charcoal shirt and black slacks he'd worn the day before. "Looks like we'll be going someplace casual," he commented, shrugging into his black bomber jacket.

Devon already had her own warm jacket on. "That's fine with me," she assured him.

"I'd like to take you someplace elegant soon," Tristan continued, giving her a smile that nearly curled her toes.

She cleared her throat and reached for her purse. "That sounds very nice. Would you mind if we take my car tonight?"

"No, why?"

"I have a meeting across town first thing in the morning and I'm almost out of gas. I meant to fill up this weekend, but *someone* kept distracting me," she said with a meaningful smile.

He grinned. "I had a delightful time distracting you this weekend."

She laughed. "I rather enjoyed it, myself."

It occurred to Devon as she pulled out of the driveway that she'd been driving each time she and Tristan had ridden in a car together. It didn't seem to bother him at all. He sat easily in the passenger seat, half-turned to chat with her. She couldn't help briefly comparing him to her ex-fiancé, Wade. Wade thought it wasn't masculine to allow himself to be driven by a woman. Funny how all Wade's macho posturing had never given him half the all-male air of confidence Tristan possessed.

She stopped at her usual station—a self-help place only a few blocks from her house—and reached for her door handle. Tristan stopped her with a hand on her arm. "Let me pump it for you," he offered.

"That's not necessary. I do it all the time."

"You've prepared several meals for me this weekend. The least I can do is pump your gas for you. Okay?"

She smiled and nodded, then couldn't resist teasing him a bit. "I thought all you Brits called it 'petrol.'"

Tristan gave her a pained look. "I've lived in the States for sixteen years, Devon. I consider myself quite Americanized now."

"Do you?"

"Quite. Now pop the bonnet, love, and I'll check your motor oil while I'm out. Would you like your windscreen cleaned, as well?"

Giggling, Devon reached beneath the dash and pulled the lever to release the car's hood.

Oh, she liked this man, she thought yet again. Very much. Dangerously much.

TRISTAN DIDN'T SPEND the night. He didn't even go back into the house with her when they returned from dinner, saying he knew she must be tired. They both needed rest, he pointed out, and then added wickedly that they wouldn't get much sleep if they shared a bed. He escorted her properly to her door, then left her with a kiss that all but melted her spine. He tore himself away with difficulty.

Devon drifted through her house in a daze, wondering at how empty it seemed without Tristan there. Had he really made himself so much a part of her life in only a weekend?

When she finally crawled wearily into bed, it was to gather the pillow he'd used into her arms and long for him to be beside her. She reminded herself that she and Tristan were only having an affair. For that matter, he hadn't said anything specific about seeing her again.

Maybe he had no intention of carrying the affair beyond this weekend.

Maybe she'd never lie in his arms again.

That thought sent a sharp pain ricocheting through her, making her flinch and curl more tightly around the pillow. For all her sensible self-warnings during the weekend, it seemed she'd come all too close to falling in love with Tristan, anyway. So much for her pose as a modern, independent woman.

Why couldn't she be more like Brandy, dammit?

But she could handle this, she told herself bravely. She'd survived the end of her engagement, hadn't she? She'd founded a thriving design business all on her own, hadn't she? She could control her feelings for Tristan Parrish, as long as she kept in mind that theirs would be only a brief liaison. She had no intention of allowing her foolish heart to ruin what could be the most exciting adventure of her sedate life. If Tristan wanted to see her again, she would be available. And when his interest waned, she'd survive. Again.

If only she were just a bit more like Brandy, she thought wistfully, drifting into sleep with the pillow still cradled against one annoyingly damp cheek.

7

"As anxious as you were to have lunch with me today, you must really be bored on your vacation," Neal Archer commented with a smile as he studied Tristan over the menu in one of their favorite restaurants. "How are you going to survive the next week and a half until you're back at work?"

Picturing Devon's lovely smile, Tristan thought he'd be very well entertained during his vacation—and afterward, for that matter. But he wasn't quite ready to go into that yet. "I'm not that bored. We always try to spend some time together when I'm in town," he remarked, glancing over his own menu.

Neal nodded acknowledgment of the point, which was, of course, quite true. Yet Tristan knew his friend still suspected there was more behind this lunch than a casual desire to spend time together. Neal knew him all too well.

They talked about their respective jobs as their meals were ordered and brought. And then, as the conversation always did, it turned to Sara, the most important part of Neal's life.

"She seems very happy these days," Tristan said, thinking of Sara's excitement-flushed, perpetually smiling face.

"She certainly seems to be, doesn't she? Did she tell you about the offer Liz made her?"

"No. What offer?"

"Liz is considering keeping her Atlanta business going and opening a second wedding-consultation business in Birmingham after she and Chance get married. The wedding's not until July, after Sara and Phillip return from their honeymoon, so Liz asked Sara if she'd been interested in taking over Special Events here in Atlanta."

"Is that right?" Tristan looked up from his lunch in interest. "Is Sara qualified to take over?"

"Well, she will receive a degree in business education in May," Neal reminded him. "She'd thought of teaching, but she's worked part-time for Liz since she was in high school. I think she'll do well at it, especially with Liz keeping an eye on her from Birmingham."

"And what does Sara say?"

"She's thrilled. She admits she'd never thought of becoming a wedding consultant, but she loves the idea. She'll be working closely with Liz on her own wedding, and Liz can be training her in other parts of the business during the next few months. I think it's going to work out."

"To be honest, I never thought Sara would have the patience to teach," Tristan admitted. "I never said so to her, of course, but can you imagine her dealing with a roomful of students who'd rather be doing anything other than attending classes?"

"I'd wondered about that myself," Neal agreed dryly. "I think Liz's idea is much better."

"So our little Sara will be a married businesswoman in a few months. Hard to imagine, isn't it?"

Neal sighed. "Yeah. Seems like yesterday I was teaching her to ride a bike and taking her to the zoo."

"You'll miss her."

Neal nodded rather grimly. "I'll miss her."

"You're a natural father, Neal. A good one. You should have more kids."

Choking on a sip of iced tea, Neal stared across the table. "You're joking, I assume?"

Tristan smiled. "Not at all."

"I'm forty years old. I've raised my child. It's up to the next generation to have more of them."

Unconvinced, Tristan shook his head. "You may feel differently when you've lived alone for a time. I think you'll be lonely."

"Now you sound just like Sara," Neal said in exasperation.

"God forbid."

Neal chuckled.

Tristan tried to think of something else to say. He wasn't quite ready to initiate the conversation they needed to have about Devon. "Are you attending that charity thing Liz is involved with this coming weekend?"

Groaning, Neal made a face. "As Sara would say, I'd rather eat a fuzzy bug than go to one of those boring events—especially this close to all the holiday socializing we've just come through. I couldn't believe they scheduled this thing just three weeks after New Year's. But, since Liz has worked so hard on it, I'd feel like a jerk not going. Maybe I'll just make a token appearance."

Grinning at the typically Sara phrase, Tristan nodded. "I know what you mean. Liz has been trying to push tickets on me ever since she found out I'll be in town that weekend."

"I wish you'd buy one. We could allow ourselves to be seen, then head for the nearest bar."

Tristan grimaced. "Nice idea, but Liz is insistent that I buy two tickets. As expensive as they are, I hate to waste the other. I'll probably take a date, if I must go." Maybe Devon would enjoy that sort of thing, he mused. She'd probably wear a beautiful gown of her own design. And it would be all he could do to behave with any sort of propriety around her during the evening, he thought with a smile.

Neal sighed. "Yeah. I've got two tickets, as well." He cut into his steak. "Maybe I'll ask Devon Fleming if she wants to go with me."

Tristan's fork clattered against his plate. "Devon Fleming?"

Looking surprised at Tristan's uncharacteristic clumsiness, Neal shrugged. "Well, she is very nice, though I don't think she was exactly bowled over with my charm and wit at dinner the other night. Maybe we should give it another try."

Tristan cleared his throat. "Neal—would you mind very much if I asked you not to invite Devon?"

Neal narrowed his eyes and very deliberately set down his knife and fork. "You want to explain?" he asked quietly.

This had to be one of the more awkward moments of his life, Tristan decided fatalistically. Though he was sure it wouldn't be necessary, the thought of having to choose between his longtime friendship with Neal and his newly discovered feelings for Devon made his stomach clench. He couldn't imagine any other woman in the world who'd be worth this risk.

How was he to begin?

"Have you ever met a woman and felt as though you'd just been kicked squarely in the chest?" he asked, remembering so clearly the moment he'd seen Devon draped in white lace and standing in a swath of sunlight.

"I can't say that I have," Neal answered thoughtfully. "Have you?"

"Only once."

"Recently, I presume?"

Tristan met Neal's eyes squarely. "Quite recently."

"We're talking about Devon?"

"Yes." Tristan drew a deep breath. "Neal, she's the most fascinating, most beautiful woman I've ever known. I haven't been able to get her out of my mind since Sara introduced us last week. And it's not as if you feel that way about her yourself—*do* you?" he asked somewhat anxiously.

"I think Devon is a very nice, very bright, very attractive woman," Neal replied. "But, no, I don't feel the way you say you do about her."

"Thank God."

Ignoring Tristan's muttered relief, Neal asked, "You could tell all those things about her just on the basis of Sara's meeting with her last Thursday?"

Tristan's throat grew tight again. Again, he cleared it. "Well, that wasn't the only time I've spent with her," he confessed.

"You've seen her since?"

Tristan had no intention of telling Neal about his inebriated arrival on Devon's doorstep Friday night. "I spent some time with her Saturday," he hedged. "And I helped her hang wallpaper yesterday."

Neal bit his lip. Tristan suspected, to his great relief, that his friend was trying to hold back a smile. "*You* hung wallpaper?"

"Yes. It was quite fun, actually." He smiled, remembering when Devon had stepped into the paste bucket. And then his smile slowly faded as he thought of the shower they'd shared afterward. Damn. He'd better stop thinking along those lines or he'd be unable to stand without embarrassing himself.

Neal leaned back in his chair and crossed his arms over his chest. "So you moved in on the woman behind my back, knowing that I'd just had a date with her Friday night?"

"It really wasn't like that, Neal," Tristan said, then winced. "Well, maybe it was like that," he corrected himself. "But—"

He sighed. "Oh, hell, Neal, I did everything I could to cut in on you. I'm sorry."

"Fortunately there's no harm done this time. Devon and I are merely friendly acquaintances. I doubt that it ever would have become anything more. The sparks just weren't there between us. But this isn't like you, Tristan."

"Tell me about it." Tristan reached up to rub the back of his neck. "I haven't been myself since I met her. She's got me tied in knots—and yet I can't wait to see her again."

"Mmm. I have to admit I'm surprised. I've never seen you this way."

Tristan smiled ruefully. "I never thought I could feel this way, either. I was wrong."

"Tristan—" Neal paused, then continued carefully "—I've only recently met Devon, but she and Liz have been friends for several years. Liz has told me quite a bit about her. Devon's a very nice person—and I meant that in the old-fashioned sense of the word. According to Liz, she's conservative, a little shy, sweet and somewhat vulnerable."

Tristan nodded. Despite Devon's delightfully eager acceptance of him during the weekend, he'd sensed from the beginning that she was usually rather introverted. He smiled as he thought of the tears in her eyes when he'd arranged the special luncheon to be served at her house on Saturday, the sentimental quiver in her voice when she'd assured him that no one had ever done anything like that for her before. What cretins the men she'd known must have been, not to realize that she was a woman made for pampering and romantic gestures!

"Did she tell you she was once engaged?"

Tristan frowned deeply. "No," he admitted reluctantly. "She didn't."

Looking uncomfortable, Neal tugged at his tie. "You know I hate gossip. I don't know any of the details—I only know that she was hurt when the guy threw her over apparently after telling her she was too old-fashioned and conservative to make a suitable wife for an up-and-coming young executive."

"The stupid bastard."

"Yeah. Liz said the guy then made a play for Devon's younger sister, who was barely out of her teens at the time. The sister wouldn't have anything to do with him, but it took Devon a while to rebuild her confidence."

"I'd love to get my hands on the son of a bitch," Tristan commented darkly, his fist clenching on his thigh. How could any sane man walk away from Devon?

"Look, I probably shouldn't have told you any of this—it is, after all, none of my business and probably not yours. I only wanted to caution you— Dammit, Tristan, I like her and she's my sister's best friend. Don't hurt her."

Tristan lifted his chin in the gesture his friends from the bar would have called his "offended-royalty pose." "I have no intention of hurting Devon."

Obviously taken aback by something in Tristan's voice or expression, Neal looked thoughtfully at him for several long, quiet moments. And then he asked, "So you really are serious about Devon?"

"Very serious," Tristan replied adamantly.

Looking both intrigued and a bit worried, Neal nodded. "Then I wish you luck."

Tristan took a deep breath as a frisson—of precognition?—shivered down his spine. Until now it hadn't occurred to him quite how vulnerable his new, powerful feelings for Devon made him. He'd never been vulnerable to a woman before. And while his family had hurt him deeply sixteen years earlier, his heart had remained relatively intact. He didn't want to think that might change with Devon.

Good luck? He just might need it. "Thanks, Neal," he said.

"I REALLY DON'T understand what you're both so concerned about," Devon said in exasperation, raising her hands palm up in a gesture of incomprehension. "I know what I'm doing."

Across the tiny restaurant table, her friends Liz and Holly shared a concerned look. And then Liz turned back to Devon, apparently trying to frame her words carefully. "Devon, we're certainly not trying to imply that you're not capable of looking out for yourself. It's just that I've known Tristan for years and while I love him dearly, he's not what I'd call the 'home-and-hearth' type. He's in Atlanta only because his employers have ordered him to take some time off. But as soon as they give him permission, he'll be off on another assignment. And then what?"

Devon tried very hard to appear unconcerned. "And then—nothing. Everything will go back to exactly the way it was before I met him. Have you ever heard me complain that I wasn't perfectly content? I do have a life, you know."

Holly looked doubtful. "I don't know, Devon. The way you were looking at him— Are you sure you aren't getting too involved?"

Devon sighed deeply. While she thought it was rather sweet that her friends were so concerned about her, she also found it a bit frustrating that they weren't giving her credit for common sense. "Holly, I was looking at Tristan the way any red-blooded woman looks at a man she finds extremely attractive. You said yourself that he's gorgeous."

Holly nodded. "Yes, he is that. Very sexy. But—"

"Then is it so inconceivable that I might simply enjoy being with him while he's in town?"

"Well, no, but—"

"I'm a grown woman, hardly an inexperienced girl. I find Tristan amusing, exciting, attractive and fascinating. I do *not* expect him to pledge undying love and devotion on the basis of a mutually satisfying vacation fling. Okay?"

Liz's lovely face creased with a frown, her dark blue eyes grave. "It just doesn't sound like you, Devon. This is the first time I've known you to engage in a 'fling' of any type, vacation or otherwise. Can you wonder that I'm concerned you'll be hurt when Tristan moves on?"

Admirably hiding a shiver of dismay at Liz's phrasing, Devon lifted her chin. "Honestly, Liz. Doesn't it even occur to you that *I* could put an end to the affair before Tristan does? That *I* could decide I really don't have the time or energy for it?"

Sure, a tiny voice whispered inside her head. *And pigs will fly.*

Sternly ignoring that annoying voice, Devon continued, "I do have a career of my own, you know. A very demanding, very fulfilling career. I don't need Tristan—or any other man—to make my life complete. But I really don't see that I have to lead the life of a nun in my rare time off."

Liz immediately responded to the offense in Devon's voice. She pushed her fine blond hair away from her face with her left hand, the light above them reflecting brightly from her antique rose-gold engagement ring with its square-cut diamond and baguettes. "Oh, Devon, I'm sorry we interfered. What you do in your time off is your own business. We really didn't mean to imply that you shouldn't have fun or that you aren't capable of making your own decisions."

"I'm sorry, too, Dev," Holly seconded earnestly. "Hey, if you're having fun with that gorgeous hunk, then I say, 'go for it.' Guess I'm just jealous. Liz is engaged to her sexy Chance and you're seeing Tristan—and I spent Friday night waxing my floors."

Devon thought of Holly's obvious distress Saturday evening at the possibility that Devon had been in bed with Neal Archer. Again she wondered if Holly's one brief meeting with Neal had really been so momentous for Holly. "So, why don't you ask someone out?" she suggested, watching Holly's expression for a reaction. "It's the modern thing to do, isn't it, rather than waiting at home for a call?"

Holly made a face. "I've asked guys out before," she replied loftily. "But just who would you suggest I ask out now? It's not like there are available men lined up on every corner, you know."

"What about Neal?" Devon asked daringly.

Holly's green eyes widened almost comically behind the lenses of her oversize round glasses. Her cheeks went scarlet. Both Liz and Devon stared at their friend in surprise, though Devon wasn't quite as startled by Holly's dramatic reaction to Neal's name as Liz appeared to be.

"Holly?" Liz prompted.

Shaking her head violently, Holly attempted a breezy laugh. "What a ridiculous idea," she scoffed just a bit too emphatically. "Neal?"

"And just what's wrong with my brother that neither of you are interested in him?" Liz demanded, looking from Holly to Devon.

Holly laughed again. "There's nothing wrong with Neal," she assured Liz. "In fact, I thought he was really attractive. But I'm hardly his type, am I? He treated me pretty much the same as he did Sara—like I was young enough to be his daughter. I think he goes for the older, more sophisticated type."

"How come you didn't think *I* was too young for him?" Devon asked in mock offense. "I'm only three years older than you are."

"Fifteen years *is* quite a difference," Liz commented. "Chance is only a couple of years older than I am. We have so much in common."

Holly choked. "You and Chance?" she asked incredulously. "About the only thing you have in common is that you're both crazy in love with each other."

Liz immediately and spiritedly started to list the many things she and her adored fianceé had discovered in common since their unconventional, five-day courtship in November.

Sitting back to listen with a smile, Devon was relieved that the conversation had turned away from her relationship with Tristan. No matter how many times she reminded herself that the affair couldn't last—that Tristan would soon be ready for another life-and-death adventure—it still hurt when other people voiced the warning.

She only hoped she'd convinced Liz and Holly that her feelings for Tristan weren't heart-deep and happiness-threatening. Unfortunately, she hadn't quite succeeded in convincing herself of that.

DEVON ALMOST FLEW to answer her door later that evening, knowing exactly who waited on the other side. Tristan stood on the doorstep, yellow roses in hand, a breathtaking smile on his handsome face. "You look lovely," he said, studying her figure-hugging cranberry silk dress in obvious approval.

Unable to stop smiling back at him, Devon stepped aside to allow him to enter. She took the flowers he held out to her and buried her face in the blooms. "Thank you. They're beautiful."

"You put them to shame," he told her, making her blush with pleasure even as she reminded herself yet again that he was very, very good at this sort of thing.

"Did you have a nice day off?" she asked him, walking toward the kitchen to put the roses in water.

He followed. "I had lunch with Neal. And I stopped by the mall and bought two new shirts. Really exciting stuff."

She smiled. "What a coincidence. I had lunch with Liz and Holly. Did you and Neal discuss anything earth-shattering?"

"Not particularly. You?'

"No, just the usual."

"Mmm." He waited only until she'd set the roses into the crystal vase she'd filled with water before turning her into his arms. "I missed you today, Devon."

Her own arms went around his neck without a moment's hesitation. "I missed you, too," she admitted.

Tristan covered her mouth with his as though it had been weeks rather than hours since he'd last kissed her. She returned the kiss with the same enthusiasm.

I think I love her, Tristan thought, pulling her slender body more tightly into his arms.

I won't let myself love him, Devon silently vowed even as she surrendered to the delights of his skillful caresses.

8

"DEVON?"

She shifted against Tristan's bare shoulder, pleasantly exhausted from their lovemaking. "Yes?"

"D'you have any plans for Friday evening?"

"No. Why?"

"It's that charity thing Liz is involved with—the one to raise money for abused children. She's told you about it, I assume?"

"Yes, of course. She's worked very hard on it, though she was sort of manipulated into serving on the committee by the mother of one of her brides."

"So that's how she became involved. Anyway, I wondered if you'd be interested in going with me. You haven't a date for it already, have you?"

She noted the sudden formality of his question—as if he would be very displeased if she did confess to having a date for the charity ball. "No, Tristan, I wasn't planning to attend. But I'd be happy to go with you, if you want me to."

He relaxed measurably beneath her cheek. "Good. It's a date, then."

"Fine."

He moved to settle her more comfortably into the hollow of his shoulder, sliding his free hand behind his head. "How does your schedule look for next week? Are you very busy?"

"I'm always busy," she answered ruefully, "but sometimes I can be flexible."

"Flexible enough to leave town for a few days?"

Her attention arrested, Devon slowly lifted her head to study his face in the shadowy light coming through the slats in the miniblinds. "Leave town?"

"Yes. I have a friend who owns an island in the Caribbean, and—"

"Your friend *owns* an island?" Devon asked in surprise.

Tristan chuckled. "A small one," he assured her. "He built a resort there. It's lovely—very peaceful, very beautiful, I understand. It's relatively new, so the tourists are only just discovering it. He's promised to make room for me anytime I want to drop in. I'd like to take you there. We could leave Saturday."

"Leave Saturday for a Caribbean island?" Devon repeated, dazed by the very idea. Things like this simply didn't happen to her!

"My holiday officially ends Wednesday week, but I could probably take an extra day or so. We wouldn't have to be back until Thursday, if you can stay that long. That would give us four full days on the island. Do you think you could arrange it?"

Trying to think clearly, Devon mentally listed the things she had to do in the following two weeks—and realized that it really wouldn't be all that difficult to arrange five or six days off. Mali was perfectly capable of handling any pressing business until Devon returned.

Her heart started to pump frantically in a combination of excitement and anxiety at the idea of going with Tristan on a Caribbean vacation.

It sounded exactly like something Brandy would do, she thought, intrigued despite the nagging warnings of her characteristic common sense.

Taking a very deep breath for much-needed courage, she said, "That sounds like a lovely idea, Tristan. I'd be happy to accompany you to your friend's island. I've never been to the Caribbean before."

"You'll love it," he promised, pulling her face to his for a quick, pleased kiss. "I'm going to show you the time of your life."

Devon ignored that disapproving little voice in her head that told her it would probably be the only time in her life she'd do anything this reckless or spontaneous.

To HIS DISSATISFACTION, Tristan saw little of Devon during the next few days. Though he knew she was working hard to clear her schedule for their impulsive trip to the island, he still begrudged every hour he had to spend away from her. Another first for him, he found himself thinking as he nursed a single beer in his usual bar on Thursday evening while Devon was busy with a client consultation. No other woman had ever consumed his thoughts so totally when he wasn't with her.

"Yo, Tris." Mitchell Drisco slid his bulky frame into the chair across the tiny round table. "Haven't seen you all week. How's the vacation coming along?"

Tristan smiled. "Quite well, actually."

"Well, you're looking better," a woman's voice said just before T. J. Harris stepped from behind Tristan and pulled up another chair. She studied his face with sharp brown eyes and nodded approvingly. "Much better. You don't look as though you're going to keel over from exhaustion or stress now."

Tristan felt obliged to protest. "One time—*one* time I give in to perfectly natural weariness and everyone acts as though I'm an aging invalid. I'll have you know I'm in perfect physical condition."

"For a man two years away from forty," twenty-five-year-old T.J. remarked complacently.

He glared at her.

"So, whatever happened to the woman you were moping over last weekend?" Mitchell inquired. "The one who was out with your best friend. Did he win the lady's favor?"

"Chauvinist pig," T.J. muttered, signaling a waitress.

Tristan lifted an eyebrow. "The lady is going with me to the Caribbean Saturday," he replied. "And my best friend approves," he added, crossing his fingers beneath the table. He wasn't actually sure Neal *would* approve of the trip, but he hoped Neal would understand that Tristan just wanted to spend more time alone with the woman he was coming to love so deeply.

Besides, Tristan intended to use those days in part to see how he and Devon fared living together. If it worked out as well as he thought it would, he intended to propose a similar arrangement once they returned. As a matter of fact, he'd found himself thinking of engagement rings, though he suspected it was much too soon to start talking along those lines to Devon. He didn't want to scare her off by moving too quickly for her.

Mitchell grinned. "Now *that's* the Tristan Parrish we all know and sort of like."

T.J. was still looking thoughtfully at Tristan. "Why do I get the feeling it's different this time?"

He returned her look without blinking. "Maybe because it is," he suggested quietly.

She tilted her head, causing her sable hair to sway against her chin. "I'd like to meet this woman."

"Yeah. Me, too," Mitchell seconded. "Say, there's a party at Hal's place tomorrow night. Why don't you bring her? All the guys from the station will be there."

"There'll even be a few print people there," T.J. added. "You know—the *real* journalists?"

Ignoring the opportunity to engage in a continuing print-versus-broadcast-news argument with her, Tristan shook his head. "Sorry. We're booked tomorrow night. We're attending that charity thing at the Marriott Marquis."

"Well, la-di-da," Mitchell teased. "Since when are you into glitzy social events?"

"Okay, so it's not my kind of thing," Tristan growled. "But it's for a good cause. And, besides," he added candidly, "I got roped into buying tickets from a friend."

T.J. sighed melodramatically. "What the women of America wouldn't give to see the 'desert dish' in a tux. Maybe I should send a photographer."

Tristan felt his cheeks warm. "Stuff it, Tyler Jessica."

Her booted foot connected solidly with his shin. "I warned you not to call me that," she reminded him when he yelped and half rose from his chair in reaction.

The timely arrival of the cocktail waitress put an end to what might have become a barroom brawl, had Tristan gone with his instincts and returned the kick. He wouldn't have, of course, he told himself later; he was too much the gentleman. But someday someone was going to have to bring Ms. Tyler Jessica Harris down a few pegs.

SOMETIME DURING the charity ball on Friday, Devon felt the strangest compulsion to look down and make sure her silver sandal heels were really touching the ground. She'd never before experienced the sensation of walking on air. Now she knew just what that old cliché meant.

She had never in her life had a more charming, more attentive or more handsome escort than Tristan. She'd taken one look at him in his beautifully tailored tuxedo and it had been all she could do not to drag him to the nearest horizontal surface and throw herself on him. Judging from the way his eyes had glazed when he'd first seen her in the clinging, backless royal-blue-and-silver sequined evening gown she'd designed herself, he'd been affected in much the same way, to her intense delight.

Tristan had hovered close to her side during the entire hour and a half they'd been at the ball, making her the recipient of more than one frankly jealous glare from less fortunate women in attendance. She and Tristan danced as though they'd been partners for years—their steps almost magically matched, his arms guiding her closely, competently across the floor.

And—most amazingly of all—she was always aware of the suitcases waiting in her bedroom, all packed and ready for an early-morning flight to a Caribbean-island resort—suitcases that held the sexy nightgowns and skimpy bikinis she'd defiantly bought herself just for this occasion, deliberately leaving out the modest cotton lingerie and conservative one-piece swimsuits she would normally have taken with her.

She'd never been happier or more excited in her life. And she'd never been more terrified.

Refusing to dwell on that nagging fear of heartbreak, she threw herself into the party with all her enthusiasm, chatting and laughing and flirting with Tristan in a manner that was wholly atypical for her. And yet it was a heady, liberating feeling, making her feel beautiful and confident and witty and interesting—the way every woman should feel at least once in her life, she thought contentedly, nestling her cheek against Tristan's broad shoulder.

His arm tightened around her waist and his steps slowed until they were hardly moving on the dance floor. Then he chuckled heartily.

She tilted her head back to look up at him in question. "What's so funny?"

He nodded toward his right. "I thought Neal and I were uncomfortable at this sort of thing, but now I see someone who's even more miserable in a penguin suit."

Following his gaze, Devon couldn't help smiling. Across the room, leaning stiffly against a white faux-marble column, Chance Cassidy frowned deeply, his hands shoved into the pockets of his plain black tux. Owner of Cassidy Construction Company in Birmingham, Alabama, Liz Archer's fiancé was a solidly built man in his early thirties with functionally-cut tobacco-brown hair, hazel eyes with deeply etched squint lines at the corners, and a tan complexion that gave testimony to a life spent primarily outdoors.

He wasn't a handsome man, exactly, and yet his own brand of rugged masculine attractiveness drew more than a few interested glances from the women around him. And he looked as out of place in this sparkly, genteel setting as a wild animal in a Victorian parlor.

"Poor Chance," Devon remarked. "Liz must be busy with her committee responsibilities. He looks miserable, doesn't he?"

"Quite," Tristan agreed dryly.

"Phillip and Sara seem to be having a good time," Devon observed, craning her neck to watch the younger couple dancing enthusiastically to the same slow, throbbing song to which she and Tristan were moving so slowly. "But Phillip really should spend some time with his brother. He has to know how uncomfortable Chance feels."

Tristan groaned as though sensing what was coming next.

Giving him a smile of apology, Devon said, "We really should go talk to him, Tristan."

Tristan sighed. "Yes, dear."

She giggled at his posturing, but firmly took his arm and headed across the floor.

Chance watched their approach with a shuttered expression. Devon knew he was still feeling his way with her; Devon and Chance hadn't exactly gotten off to a good start when they'd first been introduced. At the time, Chance had been determined to break up Sara and Phillip's engagement, thinking they were too young and inexperienced to be married.

Devon hadn't approved of Chance's interference in Sara's happiness and had made her disapproval clear. But since he and Liz had become engaged and Chance had given his blessing to his younger brother's plans, Devon had made every effort to cultivate his friendship. After all, this man would be her closest friend's husband in a few months.

"Hello, Chance," she greeted him with a smile.

"Devon," he replied politely. "You look very nice. Is that dress one of your designs?"

"Yes, it is. Thank you."

"I like the black one Liz has on tonight. She said you designed it, too."

"It does look nice on her, doesn't it? Chance, you remember Tristan, don't you?"

Chance extended his hand to Tristan. "Of course. How's it going, Parrish?"

"Couldn't be better," Tristan replied, his left hand still resting firmly at Devon's waist. "How are your wedding plans coming along?"

Chance grimaced. "Slowly," he muttered. "Liz insists on waiting until early July. I'd just as soon find a

J.P. and tie the knot tonight. This commuting back and forth between Birmingham and Atlanta is going to get very tiresome before July."

"Liz is eager for the time to pass, as well," Devon assured him. "It's just that she has so much to tie up with her business."

He nodded. "Yeah. But it doesn't make the waiting any easier."

"Waiting for me?" Liz joined them with an apologetic smile, sliding her hand under Chance's arm.

"Always," he answered, his hard face softening noticeably as he smiled down at her.

He really does love her, Devon thought in approval, studying Chance's expression. *He'll make her happy.*

Liz looked at Tristan with laughing blue eyes. "I hope you're having a better time at this affair than Chance and Neal are," she said.

He grinned and looked at Devon. "I'm having a wonderful time," he assured Liz. "Where is Neal, anyway? I haven't seen him in a while."

Liz laughed. "His date insists on dragging him out to the dance floor. You know how he hates to dance, but he's trying very hard to be a gentleman tonight."

"I don't believe I know the woman he's with," Devon said.

"She's someone he met through business," Liz explained, though without much enthusiasm. "Her name's Jean something-or-other."

"And you don't like her," Devon added.

Liz shrugged. "She's a little—pushy," she admitted.

"That's an understatement," Chance muttered. He looked at Tristan. "The woman's a real—"

"Now, Chance," Liz warned.

"—breaker," Chance finished, anyway.

Though Liz's warning had drowned out part of the expletive, Devon got the message. She frowned, thinking of nice, pleasant Neal with a woman like that. He should be with someone equally as nice, she thought. Someone like Holly.

As though he'd read her thoughts, Tristan asked, "Where's your friend Holly tonight? I haven't seen her."

Liz shook her head. "She's shooting a wedding."

Chance shifted restlessly and glanced at his watch. "How much longer do you think this shindig will go on?"

Liz patted his arm consolingly. "We can leave in about an hour," she promised.

He groaned. Devon and Tristan shared an amused glance.

Liz cleared her throat. "Are you ready to leave for your trip in the morning?" she asked, addressing the question to both of them, though she looked at Devon as she spoke.

Devon heard the worry Liz couldn't quite conceal. She knew how hard it was for Liz to accept Devon's uncharacteristic behavior. A month earlier, Devon wouldn't have believed, either, that she'd be taking off for a tropical island with an attractive, footloose reporter she'd known for only a week. But couldn't Liz understand that Devon needed to do something like this—something fun and spontaneous and daring—even if only once in her life?

"We're ready," she replied, pressing just a bit closer to Tristan's side as if to reassure herself that she was doing the right thing.

"More than ready," Tristan agreed heartily. "We'll think of you guys shivering in the winter cold while we're lounging in the tropical sun."

"No, you won't." Liz sighed. "I doubt very much that you'll think of us at all."

Tristan gave Devon a sexy, intimate smile that almost curled her toes. "No," he agreed. "Perhaps we won't."

Weakly returning the smile, Devon thought it entirely possible that she'd think of nothing but Tristan for the next few days. It was becoming increasingly difficult to ever push him far from her thoughts.

AS THOUGH IN CONTINUATION of the romantic mood the ball had inspired, Tristan made love to her very slowly, very thoroughly, very tenderly that night. One by one he pulled the pins from her hair, until it tumbled freely onto her shoulders. Inch by inch he lowered the sequined dress until her eager body was totally revealed. Little by little he drove her to the edge of madness with his hands, his lips, his tongue.

Writhing impatiently beneath him, Devon clung to his shoulders and begged him to complete what he'd started. He murmured something incoherent and slid lower, his hands separating her thighs. And then his mouth was on her, his tongue flicking against her, and Devon thought she'd go through the ceiling.

"Tristan!" Had there been any breath left in her, his name would have emerged on a scream. Instead, it was little more than a throaty gasp.

In response to her cry, he surged upward, fitting his mouth to hers at the same time he drove himself into her. "Devon," he groaned, tearing his mouth away to draw a ragged breath. "So sweet. So perfect. I— *Ahh.*"

Whatever he had intended to say faded into a harsh cry as she wrapped her legs tightly around him and hungrily met his rhythmic thrusts with her own. Their cries of release were simultaneous, echoing softly in the shadows of Devon's bedroom.

And then they rested, still locked tightly in each other's arms—no thought, no sound, no concerns allowed to intrude on their own private paradise. Nothing but each other and the way they felt, pressed cheek to cheek, heart to heart.

9

DEVON FOUND IT endearingly amusing that Tristan, with all his traveling, was a white-knuckle flier.

"If you had covered as many plane crashes as I have in the past fifteen years, you'd understand," he explained somewhat sheepishly when the trauma of takeoff was behind them and their plane was headed safely toward Miami.

"Thank you so much for that encouraging thought," she chided him, trying without much success to look concerned. She wasn't, of course. She was with Tristan. The plane wouldn't dare ruin their adventure.

Tristan gave her an apologetic smile and tightened his hand around hers. "Did you tell your mother where you'd be this week?" he asked a few moments later, as though the thought had just occurred to him.

"Of course," she replied. "I wouldn't have wanted her to worry if she couldn't get in touch with me." She didn't add that she'd been quite vague with her mother about who was going with her on this impulsive vacation. She squirmed a bit in her seat, fully aware that her mother had been left with the impression that she was making the trip with a girlfriend.

It wasn't that she had deliberately tried to deceive her mother, Devon assured herself again. It was just that it hadn't even occurred to Alice that her elder daughter would be jetting off to an island with a man she'd known less than two weeks.

"What did she say?" Tristan asked idly.

"She said she hoped I had a wonderful time."

Tristan nodded approval. "I'd like to meet your family someday. You've described them so well that I can almost picture your grandmother canning peaches and your mother coming home in the evenings from her job at the bank to tie on an apron and cook dinner."

"And my sister doing things to make my mother and my grandmother wring their hands in despair."

Tristan laughed. "I'd like to meet Brandy, too. She couldn't be that much different from you."

"Trust me. She is." Alice would have had no doubt that Brandy would be accompanied by a man on a trip like this, Devon added silently. "What about your family, Tristan?"

"What about them?"

There it was again—that odd little tone that told her she'd made him uncomfortable with her question. "Well—um—you haven't told me much about them," she pointed out carefully.

He shrugged. "Old money, even older family name. My father was a baron, and his father before him, and so on. Very proper, very traditional. I have an older brother who's a respectable barrister, husband and father, and an older sister who's a respectable wife and mother. And then there's me, the ne'er-do-well younger son. My father died wondering where he'd gone wrong in my upbringing that I'd turned out so poorly."

Her heart twisting at the old pain in his usually smiling eyes, Devon covered their joined hands with her other one. "I'm sorry, Tristan. It must be very difficult for you."

"I've learned to live with it."

"Your father was a baron?" At Tristan's nod, she asked a bit shyly, "Does that mean you should be addressed as *Lord* Parrish?"

His smile looked more like a grimace. "I'm the younger son, remember? My brother has the title. I'm only a mister."

She rested her head against his shoulder. "I really prefer misters," she said. "You're a very special man, Tristan Parrish. Your family should be proud of you."

He shook his head as though shaking off a bad memory and touched her cheek with his free hand. "You're very sweet."

Which, of course, meant that the subject was closed. Devon knew there was much more to the story—probably a particularly unpleasant event that had precipitated Tristan's estrangement from his family and his move to another country at age twenty-two. She reminded herself that a woman engaged in a temporary affair shouldn't expect to be made privy to such personal details.

That was the problem, of course. For her, at least, this was more than an affair; her feelings for Tristan more than casual attraction. She wanted to take him in her arms and comfort him, have him share his pain with her so that she could try to ease it. Yet she had no right to do so.

Refusing to give in to impending despondency, she quickly changed the subject, asking questions about the resort where they'd be staying and about Tristan's friend who owned the island, reiterating her excitement about the trip. Tristan was soon smiling again, as enthusiastic as she assured him she was.

She wasn't going to let anything ruin this time with him, Devon told herself firmly. She'd worry about learning to live without Tristan after he was gone.

"TRISTAN! IT'S GOOD to see you again."

His left arm around Devon's waist, Tristan extended his right to the man who'd called out to him as soon as they'd stepped off the tiny charter plane onto the Serendipity Island runway. "Good to see you, too, Rafe. And thanks again for making room for us on such short notice."

Tristan's friend grimaced. "It's not as though I'm fully booked yet," he explained. "The resort is just now gaining enough popularity to start showing a profit. Took me two years, but it looks like it's going to pay off."

"Glad to hear it. Rafe, I want you to meet Devon Fleming. Devon, this is Rafe Dancer, a longtime friend."

Devon was amazed at the difference Rafe Dancer's smile made to his dark, saturnine expression. Her tentatively extended hand was swallowed by a large, callused one. "Nice to meet you, Devon," Rafe said politely, studying her with interest.

Devon returned the greeting—and the inspection. When she'd first seen Rafe approaching them—his whipcord-lean body clad in a loose white shirt and white pleated slacks, his straight, jet-black hair ruffled by a light breeze—she'd thought whimsically of Mr. Roarke in the old TV series *Fantasy Island.* All he'd needed was a short sidekick at his heels.

And then he'd stepped closer and all thoughts of lightweight television fare had fled. There was nothing whimsical about Rafe's roughly-carved features or unnervingly piercing black eyes. He reminded her more of a barely tamed jungle cat than a genial resort host. She glanced at Tristan, wondering how he'd met such an unusual friend.

Tristan never stopped surprising her.

"Allow me to escort you to your cottage," Rafe offered with old-fashioned courtesy. "Don't worry about your bags—one of my staff will take care of them promptly."

Devon was sure that the service would be prompt. She suspected that Rafe's employees would be treated fairly and generously—as long as they performed to his expectations.

She was delighted when Rafe led them to a trim white open-air Jeep, and thrilled when their brief tour of the island resort proved it to be everything she'd dreamed of—palm trees, white sand beaches, neat cottages, meandering trails for walks and horseback rides, brilliant flowers, tennis courts, and swimming pools—all beneath an incredibly blue sky. Resort guests in brief, brightly colored clothing smiled and waved as the Jeep passed them, looking as though they were having a wonderful time.

She should have known it would be like this. Everything she'd shared with Tristan could have come straight from a beautiful fairy tale.

"Oh, Tristan, it's so perfect," she breathed, clutching his hand in anticipation as Rafe parked the vehicle in front of one particularly lovely little cottage overlooking a secluded cove.

Overhearing the comment, Rafe threw a grin over his shoulder. "Thank you, Devon. Tell your friends that, will you?"

"I can't wait to tell Liz all about it. What a wonderful place for a honeymoon!"

"Devon's in the wedding business," Tristan explained to Rafe, whose eyes lit up with almost-comical speculation. "She designs bridal gowns. Her friend is a wedding consultant—who would have some influence with prospective honeymoon couples," he added meditatively.

"I can't believe you didn't think of that before," Devon chided him. "You should have recommended this resort to her long ago."

"This is the first time I've seen it," Tristan replied defensively. "I haven't had a chance to get here before this."

"Still, you should have known any establishment of mine would be first-class," Rafe pointed out somewhat complacently.

Tristan sighed. "You're right. I should have. I promise I'll talk to every travel agent I know, the moment I return to Atlanta. Before long this place will be so crowded you won't even have room for old friends to pop in."

Rafe glanced over his shoulder again, his smile gone. "There'll always be room for you here, Tristan," he said, his deep voice ringing with sincerity.

Surprised by Rafe's vehemence, Devon glanced questioningly from one man to the other. To her astonishment, Tristan's cheeks had darkened, as if with embarrassment. Rafe met her gaze with an enigmatic smile. "I owe Tristan my life," he explained simply.

Tristan made a slight sound of discouragement, which didn't, of course, stop Devon from looking at him with widened eyes. "What happened?" she asked.

"It was just a matter of being at the right place at the right time," Tristan answered matter-of-factly, already climbing out of the car. "I keep telling Rafe he doesn't owe me anything."

"He took a bullet that was intended for my head," Rafe explained.

Devon covered her mouth with her hand as she thought of the jagged white scar on Tristan's right shoulder. When she'd asked, he'd told her he'd once been hurt on an assignment. And then he'd quite thoroughly distracted her attention from his scars. If she'd had any idea the scar had been caused by a bullet... She shuddered. "Oh, Tristan."

"Now look what you've done," Tristan accused Rafe, who stood by the door of the cottage, waiting to usher them inside. Tristan put an arm around Devon as he guided her up the walk. "It wasn't a serious injury and

I didn't do anything particularly heroic. I was just snooping around, looking for a story on the outskirts of a Central American revolution, when I turned a corner to find a group of guerillas surrounding Rafe, whom they'd ambushed and knocked nearly unconscious. I saw that one of them had a gun to Rafe's head and without thinking I yelled at them to stop.

"The gunman was startled into firing a shot at me, and then they scattered when they heard people shouting behind me. Rafe got me to a medic and then we went out for drinks. We got smashed and swapped war stories and we've been friends ever since. That's all of it. Does that explain everything for you?"

"Yeah. Right," Rafe muttered, making Devon suspect there was a bit more to the story than Tristan was telling her.

Tristan gave Rafe a look of warning. "That's *all*," he repeated.

Rafe nodded blandly.

Devon couldn't help smiling.

With a flourish, Rafe opened the door to the cottage and motioned them forward. Devon gasped when she stepped inside. The interior was just like an elegant suite in one of the finer hotels at home—plush carpeting, glittering lighting, deep, comfortable furniture, colorful paintings. "How beautiful! Oh, Rafe, this is lovely."

Pleased, he smiled. "Thanks. I rather favor this one. There's a stocked bar and snack refrigerator in that cabinet, which will be serviced daily," he said, indicating an intricately carved mahogany chest. "The bedroom is through that door," he added, waving toward the other side of the room.

Devon tried hard to look sophisticated, an image she knew was spoiled by the flush that stained her cheeks. She made a show of looking out the huge glass wall that dominated the back of the room, pretending to watch the waves pounding the beach below.

"Room service is available," Rafe continued, apparently missing Devon's sudden embarrassment, "but the restaurant is excellent, should you choose to dine out. We also have a lounge with live music for dancing. Occasionally I'm lucky enough to get a name performer in for a short gig, but I'm afraid you'll have to settle for the usual band while you're here. As for shopping, we have shuttles running between here and the more populated islands during the daylight hours and a launch always available if you want to go in the evenings."

"Sounds great, Rafe," Tristan said. "Thanks."

A discreet knock on the door made all three look around. "That will be your bags," Rafe explained. "I'll leave the two of you to get settled now. Don't hesitate to call me if you need anything. Understand?"

"I'll walk you to your dune buggy," Tristan offered, nodding pleasantly at the white-uniformed porter Rafe motioned toward the bedroom. "I'll just be a moment, Devon."

Devon had already started for the other room, anxious to unpack and change into suitable clothing for exploring the island.

"DEVON IS A BEAUTIFUL woman," Rafe remarked as he and Tristan walked side by side toward the white vehicle.

"Hmm. And she's quite taken, so keep your grubby paws off her."

Rafe chuckled at the mock warning in Tristan's voice, then sobered before speaking again. "She's a different type for you, isn't she? I get the impression she's not one who'd run off for a tropical tryst unless something serious was involved."

Tristan reflected with amusement that in the week or so that he'd been seeing Devon he'd been warned several times that she wasn't his usual sort of woman. What was it about her that brought out the protective instincts even of people who hardly knew her? And why was everyone so certain that he had nefarious designs on her? "There *is* something serious going on," he assured his friend. "Very serious."

Rafe smiled. "Congratulations."

Tristan smiled ruefully. "I'm not sure it's gone that far yet," he admitted. "We haven't been seeing each other very long. I'm letting Devon get used to having me around before I tell her exactly how serious I am."

"Just don't wait too long, my friend. It's best to get this sort of thing out in the open as soon as possible."

Tristan snorted. "Like you'd know about relationships!"

Rafe shrugged. "I was married once. 'I do' were about the last words we spoke to each other. Eventually, she found someone else to talk to. I learned that it takes communication to keep a relationship going, not just a good time between the sheets."

"I'll keep your advice in mind."

"Do that." Rafe climbed agilely behind the steering wheel. "Have a good time, Tristan."

Tristan grinned. "I fully intend to do just that, Rafe."

DEVON LOOKED UP HAPPILY from her unpacking when Tristan joined her in the bedroom. "Look at this room!" she enthused, sweeping a hand to indicate the king-size bed and luxury appointments. "Isn't it gorgeous? And you should see the bathroom! It's huge and almost decadently elegant. Your friend went all out on his decorating budget, didn't he?"

"Nothing but the best for Rafe," Tristan answered lightly, swallowing a sudden, unexplainable lump in his throat at the sight of Devon, sitting on the edge of the bed by an open suitcase, smiling at him with such ease. To keep his hands occupied—at least for the moment—he reached for one of his own bags, deciding he may as well get the unpacking over with. "What did you think of him?"

"Rafe?" Devon's hands paused in their work and she cocked her head thoughtfully, giving the question serious consideration. "I like him," she said slowly.

Tristan grinned. "But?"

She shook her head firmly. "No buts. I like him. I think he's a wonderfully loyal friend . . . and that he'd make a very dangerous enemy."

Tristan was pleased that Devon had summed his friend up so accurately. "You're right. He's definitely a man I'd want on my side."

"He reminds me of a barely tamed wild animal," Devon confided with a slight smile. "Like a jungle cat. Or a..."

"A wolf," Tristan supplied.

She lifted a brow. "You think of him as a wolf?"

"He once told me that his name refers to a wolf. I thought it rather appropriate."

"What was he doing in the middle of a revolution in Central America?"

"He was with the Drug Enforcement Administration at the time, I believe. I've never checked too closely into Rafe's background."

"DEA." She shivered. "Dangerous work."

"Mmm."

"I suppose you know lots of fascinating people," Devon mused, going back to her unpacking. "Rebels, revolutionaries, world leaders." Her tone was thoughtful, her expression hard to read.

"I've met a lot of people on assignments and in my travels," Tristan confirmed. "I have a lot of friends. Yet Neal and Rafe are the only two I'd trust with my life, if necessary."

"Neal?" Devon seemed intrigued. "He's very nice, but hardly the dangerous, adventurous type."

Tristan laughed and stuffed a hanger into a shirt. "You haven't seen Neal in a temper, have you?"

"You mean he has one?"

Tristan only laughed again and changed the subject. "What do you want to do first, after we get this out of the way?"

"Explore," Devon answered immediately. "I want to see everything."

He smiled indulgently. "I think that can be arranged."

Devon closed the empty suitcase and set it in a closet. "Oh, Tristan, it's just like I'd dreamed it would be," she said, giving him a shy smile that nearly turned him inside out. "Thank you for bringing me here."

His own unpacking abruptly forgotten, he caught her in his arms and pulled her close. "Thank you for coming with me," he muttered just before covering her mouth with his.

Devon locked her arms around his neck, rising on tiptoe to bring them more snugly together. Tristan closed his eyes and lost himself, as he always did, in the generous beauty of Devon's kiss.

Maybe this really was paradise, he found himself thinking, his tongue sliding slowly into the sweet depths of her mouth. He suspected that he'd be perfectly content to stay forever as long as Devon was with him.

THOUGH THE RESORT was reasonably crowded with winter-fleeing tourists, as far as Devon and Tristan were concerned they may as well have been the only ones there. They spent the next few days in a romantic haze. Uninterested in joining the island-hopping shoppers, they stayed on Serendipity, never at a loss for anything to do. They took walks—long, slow, hand-in-hand walks, their heads close together as they talked about anything and everything that occurred to them. They swam—sometimes in the clear, salty bay, sometimes in the waterfall-decorated swimming pools. They danced in the softly lit lounge, their bodies pressed intimately together. Twice Rafe joined them for dinner, but otherwise they made no effort to mingle, confining their socializing to polite smiles and passing greetings.

And they made love. Beautiful, spectacular, incredible love that fulfilled every fantasy Devon had ever had—and taught her a few things she hadn't even imagined.

There was no doubt in her mind that this was, indeed, paradise.

Toweling his hair after a shower on Wednesday morning, Tristan walked out onto the balcony of the cottage to find Devon immersed in a sketchbook at the tiny umbrella-shaded table. "What are you doing?"

She glanced up, then sighed faintly at the sexy picture he made, clad only in unbuttoned jeans, his chest and feet bare, a few sparkling droplets of water nestled among the golden hairs on his chest. She really should be accustomed to seeing him this way by now, she thought, but she suspected that Tristan would always affect her like this, no matter how long or how well she'd known him. "What did you ask?" she inquired, his question momentarily driven from her mind.

He smiled and tapped the sketchbook. "Don't tell me you're working on our vacation."

She made a sheepish face. "Well . . . only a little," she admitted. "I was inspired this morning."

"Let's see." He crouched beside her to examine the dress she'd been sketching.

The gown would have been appropriate for an island wedding. Strapless, sarong-draped, Devon had pictured it in white silk, perhaps accented with a spray of white silk orchids. The bride in the drawing wore her long hair loose and flowing, with a circlet of flowers worn like a crown. She carried a bouquet that, had Devon been using paints, would have been a glorious, multicolored cascade of tropical blooms. Devon could already imagine attendants in similarly styled, brightly colored gowns.

Tristan smiled approval. "Nice," he observed. "Not exactly traditional, but it has style."

Devon giggled, remembering his reaction to the pastel gowns in her portfolio. "What is it with you and traditional wedding gowns?"

He grinned and gave her a quick kiss. "Guess I'm just a traditional sort of guy."

"Yeah. Right." Her tone was dry with disbelief. The man was a well-known foreign correspondent, had interviewed men and women who'd shaped the world politically, had swept Devon off her feet in only hours and then carried her away to an island resort owned by a dashing ex-agent. Hardly a traditional type.

He plucked the sketchbook from her hand and dropped it on the table. "Work time's over," he informed her. "Let's go have breakfast."

She placed her hand in his and walked away from the sketchbook without a backward glance. There'd be plenty of time for her work in the days to come, she thought. But she had only one more day on this island with Tristan.

DEVON'S SILVER SANDALS dangled from her right hand. Her left hand was held tightly in Tristan's right as they strolled along the beach, listening to the roar of the waves beside them, both of them unusually quiet. It was their last night together on the island, and each was acutely aware of the swift passage of the evening.

Closing her eyes, Devon allowed herself one long, slow inhalation. She wanted to memorize the scents of moonlight-frosted, ocean-salted air, of flowers whose names she'd never learned. In the long, lonely nights to come, she wanted to be able to lie in bed, close her eyes and transport herself back to this.

"What are you thinking?" Tristan asked, his deep voice hushed in deference to the peaceful evening.

She opened her eyes and smiled at him, studying his face in the bright moonlight. "I was thinking about how perfect these past few days have been," she replied candidly.

He stopped walking to turn and face her, touching her cheek with one finger. "They have, haven't they?"

She caught his hand in hers, pressing a kiss to his palm. "Yes. Thanks to you."

He smiled and drew her closer. "That's not quite the way I see it."

Devon wound her arms around his neck, her shoes still dangling from her hand. "I wish there was no one else on the island but us," she said impulsively. "I'd like to make love to you right here, right now—lying in the moonlight with the ocean beside us and the scent of flowers all around us. And at dawn we'd lie in each other's arms and watch the sunrise."

"And then we'd make love again," Tristan added.

"Yes."

His arms tightened around her and his face went taut with need. "Devon," he said huskily, his mouth lowering to hers. "Devon, I—"

She was rising on tiptoe to meet his lips when the sound of voices intruded rudely on their fantasy. She looked around sharply to find another couple approaching down the beach, as intent on each other as Devon and Tristan had been a moment before. She sighed wistfully.

Tristan made a rough, impatient sound beneath his breath. A moment later he was moving, towing Devon in his wake as he headed for their cottage. Amused by his impatience, she hurried to keep up with him. When she stumbled, impeded by her bare feet, he turned and swept her into his arms, hardly pausing to do so. Devon clung to him breathlessly. "Tristan! You can't carry me all the way to the cottage."

"Watch me," he challenged, his wicked grin sending shivers of exhilaration down her spine. He carried her as though she weighed nothing at all, reminding her of the deceptive strength of his slender body.

She pressed her lips to his throat, just to feel the quiver of reaction in his arms.

They'd almost made it to the cottage when they met Rafe. His white suit gleaming in the soft lighting of the neatly landscaped path, he stopped walking when he saw them. And then he grinned.

"Shut up, Rafe," Tristan warned before the other man could speak.

Rafe held up both hands, palms outward. "I was only going to say good-night."

"Tell the man good-night, Devon," Tristan ordered without stopping, laughter lurking beneath his gruff tone.

"Good night, Rafe," Devon repeated obediently over Tristan's shoulder. Perhaps a month earlier she would have been embarrassed at being caught in such suggestive circumstances. But that had been the old Devon, she assured herself with great satisfaction.

"Now," Tristan said only minutes later, lowering her to her feet beside their bed. "Pretend that we are alone on the island, standing on the beach in the moonlight with the ocean beside us and the scent of flowers all around us."

Devon smiled and closed her eyes. It wasn't at all hard to pretend, she discovered. The heady scent of flowers wafted through the open window along with the muted sound of the ocean. She opened her eyes and found that she and Tristan stood in a swath of moonlight streaming through the same window. His arms were strong and firm around her, his heart beating rapidly against hers. No. It wasn't at all hard to imagine that there was no one else on the island—no one else in the world.

Sliding one arm behind his neck, she reached with her other hand for the knot of his tie. His hands immediately went to the fastening of her dress, but she stopped him with a shake of her head. "This is my fantasy," she said, easing the tie from around his neck. "Tonight I want to make love to you."

"Then, by all means—"

She covered his mouth with hers.

The kiss was long, deep and thorough. To Devon's pleasure, Tristan made no effort to take control, willingly allowing her the lead. He left his arms at his sides as she slipped his jacket from his shoulders and tossed it over a nearby chair. And then she went to work on the buttons of his silk shirt, pausing after every other one to press a kiss to his chest as she gradually bared it.

When the shirt, too, lay across the back of the chair, Devon allowed herself a leisurely reexploration of the masculine torso she'd come to know so well in the past two weeks. She started with the scar on his shoulder— the scar she now knew had been obtained by courageously risking his life to save a stranger's. She traced the crooked, three-inch line with a finger and then the tip of her tongue. Tristan shifted restlessly.

She moved down his chest, licking first one flat brown nipple and then the other. She used the edge of her teeth very carefully on one nub, making Tristan jerk in reaction. His fists clenched at his sides, the muscles standing out sharply in his upper arms. Devon smiled against his skin, sliding one hand slowly down his side to the waistband of his slacks. And then lower.

He was fully aroused beneath the expensive fabric. She stroked him, measuring his length with her fingertips, then taking him in her palm to gently squeeze.

Tristan groaned huskily. "Ah, Devon, you can't possibly know what you're doing to me."

She sank to her knees, her fingers searching out his zipper. "Oh, I think I have an idea," she murmured. The zipper rasped harshly, the sound just audible over Tristan's ragged breathing.

A moment later his breathing seemed to stop completely.

Tristan could hardly think coherently by the time Devon placed her hands on his chest and pushed lightly, pressing him back onto the bed. Dazed and utterly delighted by this new, daring side of her, he tried to pull her down with him. She gave him an unsteady smile and shook her head, reaching behind her neck for the fastening of her halter-top evening gown. Only then did he realize that, while he was completely nude, Devon still wore everything but her shoes.

Holding his eyes with hers, she finally released the straps of her gown, baring her breasts. Hot and hungry for the sight of her, he lowered his gaze slowly. She was so beautiful, her soft, full mounds silvered by the moonlight, the rosy tips berry-hard, ready for his touch. The gown slid lower and she gave a sexy little wriggle to free her hips. Tristan swallowed a groan, not at all certain he'd survive the night, and not particularly concerned about the possibility that he wouldn't.

When the last of her garments had been removed, she finally stepped forward, lowering herself to the bed beside him. Tristan reached eagerly for her. Again she evaded his arms.

"Devon," he growled, patience thinning. "I can't take much more of this."

She leaned over him, the tips of her breasts just brushing the hair on his chest, her smiling mouth only inches from his. "Does that mean you want me to stop?"

"No. God, no." He raised his head to join their mouths, his tongue plunging deeply into her smile.

She was liquid heat in his hands, flowing over him, around him until he thought he'd go up in flames. His skin burned beneath her hands, which seemed so arousingly cool in contrast. He had almost reached the point where he'd have been willing to beg by the time she finally straddled him. As she lowered he thrust upward, joining their bodies smoothly, fluidly. And then they leaped into the flames together, burning away all rational thought in the process.

TRISTAN COULDN'T have said how much time had passed when he finally opened his eyes. Devon lay bonelessly on top of him, her moist skin pressed against his. He dropped a kiss on the top of her head, then shifted her to lie at his side, within the circle of his arm.

He couldn't think of a better time to tell her how he felt about her. "Devon?" he murmured, turning his head to look at her.

She was asleep. Sound asleep, her mouth tilted into a slight smile, her hand lying gently on his heart.

He smiled, kissed her forehead and closed his eyes. She surely knew how he felt, anyway, he thought contentedly. How could she not know that he loved her after these perfect days in paradise?

10

WITH AN EAGERNESS that would have been amusing had it been anyone but himself, Tristan started his classic British sports car and guided it out of the television station's parking lot. It was Friday evening—nearly twenty-four hours since he'd last seen Devon—and he was doing everything but counting the minutes until he had her in his arms again. "You're truly hooked, old man," he told his reflection in the rearview mirror.

The man in the mirror didn't look particularly concerned.

Tristan almost groaned as he thought of the flight he had to catch first thing next morning. His producer had hardly taken time to welcome him back to work before giving him an assignment that would send him to Africa for the next several weeks. Africa. A very long way from Devon, he thought with a sigh.

Maybe Neal was right. Maybe it was time for Tristan to turn the globe-trotting and story chasing over to the younger guard. It wasn't as though he had no other options. More than once, he'd been offered anchor positions with his current cable-news employer and with the national networks. A national news-magazine program had been after him since the Gulf War to take a regular spot on their staff. He'd even had print offers—an influential friend in publishing had urged him to write a syndicated column, and another had suggested that he write a book based on his reporting experiences.

There were all sorts of avenues open to him, he realized, that would allow him to live a normal family life and still be employed in a career he enjoyed.

Perhaps he would discuss them with Devon this evening. He knew she had career plans of her own, dreams of seeing her line of clothing in the most prestigious stores. Together they could decide whether Atlanta was the most advantageous base for them. He didn't particularly care where they lived, as long as it was together.

He'd missed sleeping with her last night. But they'd arrived home tired and rumpled, in need of showers and rest. Both had unpacking to do, mail and messages to check, calls to make. They'd separated at her door with one long, lingering kiss. Tristan had thought Devon's eyes looked sad when he'd pulled away, but she'd claimed weariness and sent him on his way with an almost-natural-looking smile.

They hadn't actually made plans for this evening. He'd meant to call during the day, but there simply hadn't been a spare moment. Perhaps he was taking for granted that she'd be free, that she'd be expecting him to show up at her door, he reflected with a sudden frown. But then he shook his head and assured himself that of course she'd be free. Devon was as committed to this relationship as he was. After all, she'd just spent four and half days in paradise with him.

He pressed a bit harder on the accelerator, unwilling to waste another moment without her. He felt rather like an infatuated schoolboy; wouldn't his friends from the bar laugh if they could see him? But, damned if he cared.

Devon opened her door to him with a smile. "Tristan! Come in."

He entered, eyeing her questioningly. "You sound as though you're surprised to see me."

"Well, we didn't actually make plans for this evening," she pointed out. "But I'm glad you're here."

He reached out to snag her waist and pull her closer. "And where else would I be?" he asked simply, before taking her mouth with a hunger that had grown to ravenous proportions during the past twenty-four hours without her.

Devon returned the kiss with the same generous eagerness that had gotten him hooked on her kisses in the first place. Tristan felt the impact all the way down to his heels. This was what had been missing in his life before, he thought contentedly. Someone to come home to.

Devon's smile wasn't quite steady when he finally released her. "Are you hungry?" she asked somewhat huskily. "I was planning a pasta, spinach and crab casserole for dinner, but I can make something else if you'd prefer."

"That sounds great. What can I do to help?"

"Just keep me company while I put it together. Would you like something to drink?"

He followed her into the kitchen. "A hot cup of tea sounds good. I haven't acclimated back to winter weather yet."

She laughed as she filled the teakettle and placed it on a burner. "I know how you feel. I've shivered all day and it really isn't that cold. Just cool and damp."

"So you didn't feel like slipping into a bikini and lying out in the sun today, eh?"

Grimacing, she opened the refrigerator door and began pulling out the ingredients for her casserole. "What sun?"

Tristan pulled a chair from beneath the kitchen table and straddled it backward, his chin propped on his crossed hands as he watched her work. "How was your day? Everything back to normal?"

She sighed deeply. "I don't know if you can call it normal. Frustrating, maybe."

"Oh? What happened?"

"Remember the gown I had on when you surprised me with a visit the day after Sara introduced us?"

"How could I forget?" He could still clearly picture her in that gown, just as he could remember the physical impact the image had made upon him. He'd probably started to fall in love with her at that moment.

"Well, the bride, Sheila, was to have been married tomorrow evening."

"Past tense?"

"Past tense," she confirmed with a sober nod. "Apparently she got cold feet earlier this week and backed out. Liz has been running herself ragged trying to cancel all the orders, get refunds where possible, collect the bills that Sheila will have to pay, anyway."

"And what about the gown?"

Devon rolled her eyes. "Sheila called first thing this morning to see if she could get a refund. She's been bugging Mali about it all week, but of course Mali told her she'd have to wait until I returned for an answer. Normally I wouldn't give a refund on a custom-tailored dress, particularly at the last minute like this. But with this gown . . ."

She paused, shrugged, then smiled ruefully. "I couldn't bear the thought of it being shoved to the back of a closet, or sold through a newspaper ad. I really think it's one of the most beautiful gowns we've ever done. So I'm giving her back her money."

"All of it?" Tristan asked with a frown. Devon deserved something for the hours of work that had gone into the gown. She'd probably sell it eventually, but still—

"I'm deducting a fee for my trouble. She'll be getting a bill from Liz, as well. Sheila really should have decided sooner that she wasn't ready to be married."

"How'd her fiancé take her decision?"

"Liz said he was devastated. He really loves Sheila, apparently. He tried to get her to change her mind, but Liz said she won't even talk to him."

"Poor bastard."

"I really didn't know them very well, but Liz said she wasn't really all that surprised when Sheila called her. She always thought Sheila was a little flaky."

Tristan's thoughts had already turned back to the gown. He remembered how beautiful Devon had looked in it. He wondered if her affection for it was personal enough that she'd want to be married in it, herself. Or did she have other plans for her own gown? Which led, of course, to thoughts of another wedding—his and Devon's. He glanced around the room before noting the distracted look on Devon's face as she slipped the casserole into the oven. Maybe this wasn't the best time to mention marriage, he decided, telling himself to be patient. A woman like Devon deserved hearts and flowers, music and romance, not an impulsive proposal in the kitchen.

"Devon . . ."

He wasn't exactly sure what he would have said in that moment. Maybe he'd have told her that he loved her: that coming home to her, sitting in the kitchen sipping tea while she made their dinner made him so happy his chest ached with the overflow of emotion.

Whatever he might have said was abruptly cut off when the telephone rang. With a smile of apology to him for the interruption, Devon answered it. "Hello? Oh, hi, Holly. Yes, we had a wonderful time."

Half-turned away from Tristan, she finished dinner preparations as she and Holly chatted for a few minutes, first about Devon's vacation, then about the canceled wedding that had Liz, Holly and Devon so inconvenienced.

Tristan took another sip of his tea and listened unabashedly to Devon's end of the conversation, still basking in his contentment. Okay, he thought with a crooked, secret smile, so maybe he *was* behaving like a man straight out of a 1950s situation comedy. He'd try to restrain himself before he started thinking of Devon as 'the little woman.' Something told him she'd make her displeasure with that little gaffe quite painfully clear. Despite her delightful domesticity, Devon was very much a modern self-sufficient woman. Exactly his type of woman.

Devon hung up the phone and turned to smile at Tristan. "That was Holly."

"I got that impression. How is she?"

"Still very envious about our vacation."

"And so she should be."

"Mmm." Devon's smile was so dreamily reminiscent that Tristan had to forcibly restrain himself from tossing her over his shoulder and carrying her to the bedroom. He reminded himself sternly that there was more to this relationship than sex.

Pouring herself a cup of tea, Devon joined Tristan at the table. "You haven't told me about your day," she reminded him. "Were you glad to get back to work?"

Which, of course, reminded him that he still hadn't told her about his new assignment. He grimaced. "I am definitely back at work. I leave first thing in the morning."

Devon went still, her eyes locked on his face. "You leave in the morning? For where?"

"I'm covering an insurrection in a tiny African country most people have never even heard of. In a week or so, almost everyone will know about it. It's going to get ugly."

"Africa," Devon repeated hollowly. She cleared her throat. "Will it be dangerous for you?"

He squirmed guiltily, remembering all the times he'd flown off into risky situations without a second thought. Though Neal and other friends had told him they worried about him, it had never been brought home so clearly exactly how his recklessness had affected those who cared about him—maybe because there had been so many years when no one at all had cared.

Perhaps he should give Neal a call tonight and thank him for worrying in the past. And then he almost grinned. Neal would think he'd lost his mind.

"I'll be careful," he promised Devon.

"Sure," she said with a weak smile. "Just like you always are."

"No, really," he insisted. "I'll take care." This time he had something very important to come home to. A very special reason to stay in one piece.

Devon looked into her tea as if trying to see the future there. "I hope you will," was all she said.

The silence between them grew awkward. Tristan wondered what, exactly, was wrong. Was Devon upset that he was leaving? Worried about his safety? Maybe now was the time to tell her about the other career avenues he was considering. But, before that, he'd better warn her what to expect from the next few weeks.

"Devon, I wish I knew exactly when I'd be back in Atlanta, but I'm afraid I can't even give a guess. This could last anywhere from a few days to several months.

And as far as communication— Well, I'll be lucky to get calls out to my producers. As for mail—"

She interrupted with a bright, patently false smile. "Please, Tristan, there's no need to explain. I understand perfectly."

There was something in her tone that he didn't care for at all. He'd been on the verge of explaining that he didn't know how dependable the mail service would be, but that he'd find a way to get letters and messages to her, whatever it took. Instead, he asked carefully, "You understand *what* perfectly?"

"Well, about how busy you are on assignment. I'm sure it takes all your concentration just to stay out of danger while you're pursuing your story."

He truly disliked the breezy, chatty way she was speaking. Whatever had gotten into her? "Devon . . ."

Without looking at him, she pushed herself away from the table and started rummaging in the pantry. "Dinner should be ready in a few minutes. I took some of my grandmother's wheat rolls out of the freezer this morning, so all I have to do is pop them in the oven to brown. Do you like fruit compotes?"

This was getting weird, Tristan decided. It was as if his Devon had suddenly been taken over by someone else, someone he didn't know at all. "Devon, about my trip. As I said, I don't know exactly when I'll be back—"

"I know. I'll watch for your reports every evening. I'm sure they'll be as fascinating as your stories always are."

"Dammit, Devon—"

She turned and looked at him with a bland smile that stopped his words in his throat. "I want you to know that it's been a wonderful two weeks, Tristan. Thank you for taking me to Rafe's island. I've never had a more delightful vacation."

"What the hell—"

He could have snarled in frustration when he was interrupted yet again, by the peal of her doorbell this time. Before he could order her to ignore it—which was exactly what he'd intended to do—she had hurried out of the kitchen.

"Damn it to hell." He slammed one fist into the palm of his other hand. What was going on? Why was Devon acting this way? *Why had she sounded as if she'd been saying goodbye?*

His jaw hardening with determination, he stormed after her.

He found her in the living room with a strikingly attractive, artfully sun-streaked blonde whose luscious curves were outlined by a skintight sweater and a just-long-enough-to-be-legal leather skirt. "Oh, my," the blonde exclaimed when Tristan entered. "And who is this beautiful man?"

Devon sighed audibly. "Brandy, try to remember your manners, will you?"

Tristan cocked his head in interest. "So this is your sister," he remarked, studying the young woman more closely. Right away he could see that Devon hadn't been exaggerating about the differences between herself and her younger sister. As far as he could tell, they were direct opposites.

Brandy smiled and stepped closer to Tristan with an outstretched hand. "I'm Brandy Fleming. And you are . . . ?"

"Tristan Parrish," he supplied, taking the soft, long-nailed hand in his. Her fingers promptly curled around him, clinging when he would have released her.

"Tristan Parrish," Brandy repeated thoughtfully. And then her dramatically made-up eyes brightened. "You're the TV reporter!"

"You mean you've actually watched the news network?" Devon asked her sister in apparent surprise.

Brandy laughed musically. "I read an article about you in *People* not long ago," she explained to Tristan, ignoring Devon's question. "Your pictures didn't do you justice."

"Thank you. I think."

She laughed again and moved a few inches closer. "However did you meet Devon? I didn't think my sister moved in such distinguished circles."

Tristan lifted a brow. "Your sister has made quite a name for herself with her designs. In some circles her name would be better recognized than my own."

"Chivalry. How sweet," Brandy murmured. "Do I smell dinner cooking, Devon? You always were such a good cook. Just like Grammie. I'm hopeless in the kitchen, myself," she added with a smile for Tristan. "I just never seemed to have the time to concern myself with measuring flour and butter."

"Brandy, why are you here?" Devon asked bluntly.

Brandy looked meaningfully at Tristan before glancing back at Devon. "Why don't I help you set the table and we'll discuss it? I'm sure you made enough for one more to join you, didn't you? Tristan, you don't mind, do you? I haven't seen my sister since Christmas. I understand she's been out of the country for the past week on a little vacation with a friend."

Tristan wondered at Brandy's wording. "She and I got back from the Caribbean yesterday," he confirmed. "We had a fabulous time, didn't we, love?"

Devon's cheeks went pink at the endearment, but she still refused to meet Tristan's questioning gaze. Instead, she grudgingly agreed that Brandy could join them for dinner. "As long as you behave yourself," she added sternly.

Brandy giggled. "Honestly, Dev, now you even *sound* like our grandmother."

"I'll just wash up for dinner now," Tristan said hastily, when Devon's eyes narrowed. It was going to be a very interesting evening, he decided, running a finger around the collar of his shirt. How had it degenerated so quickly from blissful contentment to this?

DEVON STEPPED INTO the kitchen and covered her face for a moment with her hands. What a horrible evening! A surprise visit from Brandy had been all she'd needed on top of Tristan's announcement that he was leaving early in the morning for Africa. She'd known it was coming, of course, just as she'd expected his vague explanations that he wouldn't be able to stay in touch with her. Hadn't she known all along that she was merely a vacation diversion for him? Something to do until he was back at the job he loved?

She'd give him credit, at least, for breaking it off smoothly and gently. And, if she weren't hurting quite so badly she'd be proud of herself for handling the announcement as well as she had. She hadn't protested, hadn't begged, hadn't caused a scene—just the way a modern, sophisticated woman was supposed to react at the end of a fleeting affair.

But, oh, God, how it hurt!

"You okay, Dev?"

At Brandy's less-than-solicitous question, Devon lifted her head and glared at her younger sister. "All right, Brandy, why are you here? Why did you invite yourself for dinner?"

Brandy busied herself checking her nail polish. "I wanted to stay for dinner because I'd like to get to know Tristan better," she explained. "I've never met a famous TV reporter before. Can you blame me for finding him interesting?"

"Why are you here?" Devon asked for the third time, refusing to acknowledge the other explanation.

Brandy sighed and let her hand fall to her side. "All right, Devon, I'm here because I'm in trouble. My stupid boss fired me from my job, just because she never liked me, and now I've got bill collectors calling me up and making all kinds of ugly threats and noises. I guess I could've asked Mom for a loan, but—"

"Don't ask Mom," Devon interrupted wearily. "I'll lend you some money until you find another job."

Brandy smiled brightly. "I knew you'd come through. Thanks, Dev."

"You're welcome. The plates are in the cabinet to the right of the refrigerator."

"Plates?"

"You're helping me set the table, remember?" Devon prodded, knowing full well that Brandy hadn't had any such intention. She slipped her hands into oven mitts and reached inside the stove for the casserole and rolls.

Without enthusiasm, Brandy opened the cabinet door and pulled out three plates. "You know, I'm surprised at you, Devon. Don't you think you're a little old to be fibbing to Mom about who you spend your vacations with?"

Devon set the hot casserole dish on a trivet with a thump. "I did *not* fib to Mom. I told her I was going on vacation with a friend. I didn't mention Tristan's name simply because she's never met him and she may have worried about me going out of the country with a man who's a stranger to her."

"So, how did you meet him?"

"We were introduced by mutual friends."

"I have to admit I'm surprised that the two of you seem so cozy. He hardly seems your usual type."

"And just what is my usual type, Brandy?"

"Oh, you know. Average. Unadventurous."

"You mean dull," Devon interpreted.

Brandy smiled and shrugged. And then her expression grew serious. "Devon, do you mind if I offer a little advice? I mean, let's face it, I've had more experience with men like Tristan."

"Brandy—"

"Really, Dev, I just don't want you to get hurt. I know you. You're probably thinking about wedding rings and picket fences and babies, but men like Tristan just don't go for that sort of thing. I mean, what is he—thirty-eight? Forty? And, according to *People*, he's never been married or even involved with any particular woman for more than a brief time between assignments. That should tell you something about him."

"Brandy, it really isn't necessary to warn me about Tristan's intentions—or lack thereof. I know exactly what to expect from him."

"Just as you thought you knew what to expect from Wade. Right?"

Devon bit her lip at the catty reminder of her broken engagement. "That was low."

Brandy had the grace to look somewhat contrite. "I know. I'm sorry," she said with uncharacteristic sincerity. "I guess it just took me by surprise to find you with Tristan and to find out that you've been away with him. You've always been so conservative, so old-fashioned about things like this."

"So dull," Devon supplied again, her serrated emotions merging into a spurt of temper. "Well, maybe it's time for you and everyone else to realize that I'm not a shy virgin longing for some nice, settled man to marry me and give me a life. I *have* a life, Brandy. Maybe it's not as reckless or adventurous as yours, but I'm perfectly happy with it. I have a career that I love and that I'm doing well in, good friends to spend my time with, I own my own home and make enough money to be totally self-sufficient. I thank heaven every day that I didn't marry Wade.

"As for Tristan, he's a very attractive, very interesting man. We've had fun, but that's all there is to it. What makes you think I'd even *want* more than that from him?"

"Well, I—"

"You certainly haven't tied yourself down to any one man, have you, Brandy?" Devon demanded, knowing full well that her sister avoided emotional commitments as fervently as a hypochondriac avoided germs. "Yet I notice that you don't mind their company."

"I'm certainly not interested in getting married or having kids—at least, not for years yet," Brandy admitted. "But I enjoy being with good-looking, amusing, interesting men."

"Exactly," Devon said with relish. "What woman wouldn't enjoy a pleasant little fling on a tropical island with a fascinating man?"

"None that I know," Brandy replied, grinning at Devon in rare consensus.

"Me, neither." Devon tried to return the smile naturally. She tried to tell herself that she'd accomplished her goal of adding some excitement and adventure to her life. Brandy, at least, would no longer think of her as the "good girl." So why didn't that make Devon feel any better about the end of her affair with Tristan?

Probably because it had always been more than just an affair. From the beginning, it had been a *love* affair.

A slight sound from the doorway made Devon look up with a start to find Tristan watching her. Something about his expression made her chest tighten. How much had he overheard? And why did he look so grim? She'd thought he'd be relieved to have confirmation that Devon wouldn't be clinging to him when he left, that she wouldn't expect anything from him when he returned. After all, hadn't he been trying ever so delicately to determine that before Brandy arrived?

Clearing her throat, she looked quickly around to check what remained to be done before serving dinner, only to find the three plates Brandy had removed from the cabinet still sitting on the counter. "Brandy, you haven't even started to set the table," she reminded her sister lightly, almost feeling Tristan's gaze burning into her. "You grab the plates and utensils and I'll bring the food. Here, Tristan, you carry the rolls."

Tristan complied without a word, his movements unusually stiff, his natural gracefulness conspicuously absent. Devon suppressed a sigh, wondering what else could possibly go wrong this evening.

BRANDY DIDN'T LINGER after dinner, staying only long enough to tuck a generous check from Devon securely into her purse. Even though it had visibly disappointed Brandy that Tristan hadn't responded to her speculative flirting during dinner, she left him with a warm smile and a suggestion that he give her a call sometime. "I'd just love to hear more about your fascinating job," she'd added in a seductive murmur. Tristan had said something appropriate and told her it was nice to meet her. Brandy left with a smile and a you-can't-blame-me-for-trying shrug for Devon.

The silence in the wake of Brandy's departure was so heavy Devon could almost feel it enclosing her, smothering her. She risked a peek at Tristan, finding his expression set and distant, and a pale line around his mouth that she'd never noticed there before. "Tristan? Is something wrong?" she asked hesitantly.

He shook his head curtly. "I'd better be going. My plane leaves very early in the morning."

She made an impulsive grab for his arm when he would have walked past her. "Tristan, please. What is it?"

The look he gave her made her fall back, dropping her hand to her side. "It was nice to hear that you enjoyed our 'pleasant little fling on a tropical island.'"

She flinched from the barely suppressed violence in his voice. "You heard me talking to Brandy."

"Yes. It was quite illuminating. Tell me, Devon, whatever made you think that all I wanted from you was an affair—a 'fling'?"

"I've always known," she answered blankly. "I mean, everyone knows that you're not interested in anything more serious, that you aren't interested in commitments."

"Ah, yes. Everyone knows that." His words were clipped. His eyes were dark and angry.

"I thought you were different," he said after another moment of taut silence. "I thought you looked at me and saw something no one else could see. But you're no different from the others, are you, Devon? No different from my family. You made up your mind about me before you even met me, and nothing I've done since has changed your preconception."

"Tristan!" Devon followed him onto the porch, trying desperately to understand what was going on. "You're so angry because I called our relationship a pleasant fling?"

He stood by his car, digging into his pocket for his keys. "Bloody right," he growled, opening the driver's door.

"Well, what the hell would you have called it?" she demanded irritably, stunned that he was leaving her this way.

He paused with one foot already in his car, his expression bleak. "I'd have called it a courtship," he said finally.

He was in the car and out of the driveway before she could emerge from her shock and ask for an explanation.

11

ON THE FIRST FRIDAY afternoon in February, Devon looked up from her sketchbook to check her watch. Sara was late again. For her first fitting, this time.

Her chin propped in her hand, Devon stared listlessly at nothing and remembered that it had been four weeks since Sara had introduced her to Tristan. Who could have dreamed how much Devon's life would change in just four short weeks?

Nothing in her life had ever hurt as much as losing Tristan. No matter how determinedly she'd tried to prepare herself, no matter how many times she'd warned herself that it wouldn't last, she was still devastated. She hadn't slept a full night since he'd left—missing him, aching for him, so painfully aware of how empty her bed and her life were without him.

And she was haunted by questions that simply wouldn't go away, couldn't be ignored for more than a few moments at a time. Had she driven him from her by misjudging his intentions? Had she hurt him by not believing in him?

"I thought you were different. I thought you looked at me and saw something no one else could see. But you're no different from the others, are you, Devon? No different from my family."

She could still hear his words as clearly as though he were standing in front of her, hurling them at her again. She covered her face in a vain attempt to hide from the memory.

She'd known there was something in his past that had hurt him, something that had driven him from his home, his country. What had she done to remind him of that old pain? And what, exactly, had he meant by his parting words?

"I'd have called it a courtship."

A *courtship* in Devon's vocabulary referred to a relationship headed for the altar, for marriage and family and happily-ever-after. Yet Tristan had never indicated that he was thinking along those lines with her. Not even when they'd made love had he said anything to lead her to believe there was more between them than a fiery physical attraction. How was she to have known that he was considering marriage—if that was what he'd meant by "a courtship"?

During the past two long, lonely weeks since he'd left, Devon had reached one very clear conclusion: She wasn't cut out for fleeting affairs, for a life of risk and adventure. She'd tumbled head over heels in love with the first exciting man to sweep into her life and she wanted nothing more than to marry him and spend the rest of her life with him. She couldn't even imagine ever being with another man; cringed from the thought of sharing herself with anyone other than Tristan. And she bled at the image of Tristan making love to anyone but her.

She had been so very wrong to try to be someone other than herself. By comparing her life so harshly to Brandy's, Devon had lost sight of the fact that she'd been quite content as she was; that her goals, her desires, were very different from Brandy's. Brandy wanted variety, adventure, money, flash. Devon wanted a successful career, a home and a family; a husband, children, commitments and permanence.

Had she lost her one chance at having those things by refusing to look beneath the surface of Tristan's flattering attentions?

She blinked hard against threatening tears, refusing to give in to them again. She'd shed more tears in the past two weeks than she had in the past four years combined.

The doorbell provided welcome relief from her thoughts. She pushed her hands through her loose hair and went to answer the summons, praying that Sara would be too excited about trying on her dress to mention Tristan during the appointment.

She should have known better, of course.

Sara adored the dress, even though it was little more than a silk underslip at the moment. The lace, beading, appliqués, bow and portrait collar would be added after the fitting was complete. "It's perfect." Sara sighed, stepping out of the garment. "Just perfect."

Devon smiled. "A little plain at the moment."

"Yes, but I can already picture it with the frills added. It's going to be the most beautiful gown ever."

"That's what I want every bride to say." Devon slipped the dress onto a padded hanger and hung it on a rack.

Already back in her jeans and sweater, Sara idly flipped through the other dresses hanging in the room in various stages of completion. She stopped when she came to one gown hanging alone in a clear plastic covering. "Oh, Devon. How gorgeous!"

Devon looked up, then almost flinched as memories flooded her. Sara was studying the wedding dress Devon had been wearing the day Tristan surprised her. This gown had been special to Devon from the beginning, for some reason. Now it hurt to even look at it. "Um—thank you, Sara. That's the one Sheila Hankins was to have worn."

Sara rolled her eyes expressively. "That is one messed-up space cadet," she said. "The way she put everyone through the wringer—especially her poor fiancé—she didn't deserve a gown this beautiful, anyway."

Studying the dress more closely, she shook her head. "It's just incredible. Look at this beading, the pattern of these stones. Devon, it's so beautiful. You should have it featured in one of those bridal magazines."

Devon was beginning to worry that Sara liked the dress better than her own. As though she'd read Devon's mind, Sara glanced over with a smile. "It's really not my style, of course. I'd look like a kid playing dress-up in a gown this elaborate. But someone taller and slimmer, someone classy enough to . . ." Her candid words trailed off reflectively and her gaze became speculative. "This dress would look perfect on you."

Devon's smile wavered. She forced it in place. "On me?"

"I can picture you so clearly in this gown. It would be ideal."

Busying herself with gathering her tape measure and straight pins, Devon faked a laugh. "Maybe we'd better just concentrate on your wedding, for now. How are your other plans coming along? Have you decided on the menu for your reception yet?"

"Mmm. Have you heard from Tristan since he left, Devon?"

Devon swore as a straight pin jabbed into the end of her finger, drawing a scarlet drop of blood. She wrapped it quickly in a tissue snatched from a conveniently located box. "No, Sara. I haven't heard from him."

"Oh. Neither has Daddy. In fact, Daddy wondered why Tristan didn't even call him before he left. Usually he does."

Avoiding Sara's eyes, Devon tried to speak nonchalantly. "Does he?"

"Mmm. Have you seen his reports?"

"Yes." She'd haunted the television set every evening, waiting for glimpses of Tristan, hurting each time she'd seen him, hardly able to concentrate on the grim events he was covering.

"He looks terrible, doesn't he? Daddy and I are getting worried about him. He's looked tired before, but this story must be the most difficult he's ever done, judging from his appearance. So thin and pale and exhausted. Even the anchor commented on it last night."

Devon had heard. The concerned anchor had explained that the on-site crew had been dodging from cover to cover in the country that, in its present turmoil, did not welcome foreigners—particularly reporters. They'd had little sleep, their food was running low, they were relying on generators and battery packs for power sources for their transmissions. A cameraman from a British reporting team had disappeared only the day before, taken by government soldiers who'd been filmed beating an unarmed captured rebel.

Even if Devon hadn't been suffering so deeply over the end of her affair with Tristan, she'd still be living in hell, worrying about his safety. Even if Tristan had wanted a permanent relationship with her, she'd have had to seriously think about whether she could live with this job of his, his tendency to endanger his life for a story.

Not that it would have made a difference in her decision, she reflected with a small sigh. If Tristan had wanted a commitment from her, she'd have given it. No second thoughts. No conditions. She loved him. Somehow she'd have learned to live with the fear—just as she'd have to learn to deal with it now. Regardless of the way they'd parted, she still couldn't bear the thought of anything happening to him.

Realizing that Sara was still waiting for a response, Devon cleared her throat. "Tristan's been in dangerous situations before. He's very good at taking care of himself," she tried to say bracingly.

"He just looks—I don't know—different this time," Sara mused, still watching Devon. "Like maybe there's something else bothering him?"

Sara had done everything but come right out and ask what was going on between Devon and Tristan. Devon suspected that would come next. Sara, of course, knew that Devon and Tristan had been away together and would naturally be curious about what had happened afterward. Devon met the younger woman's eyes, knowing her distress would be apparent in her own. "Sara, I really can't talk about this now, okay? Tristan and I…didn't part very well. So would you mind if we changed the subject?"

Instantly contrite, Sara took Devon's hands in her own, impulsively pressing her cheek to Devon's. "I'm sorry. I didn't mean to hurt you by prying. I'm only concerned about you. About both of you."

"I know you are." Devon tried again to smile. "I'm lucky to have such good friends as you and Liz and Holly."

Liz and Holly knew, of course, that Devon was hurting, that the affair with Tristan hadn't ended happily. But even with them, Devon had been unable to open up; had said only that she wasn't yet ready to talk about it. They'd understood, offering endless love and support, which meant so much to Devon.

Sara didn't stay much longer, saying she knew Devon must be busy. She left with another warm hug, telling Devon again how much she loved her gown.

Devon fought tears after Sara left, finally warding them off by throwing herself into her work. Tears threatened again when she came across the drawing in her sketchbook of the island-inspired wedding dress. Again, it took all Devon's fortitude to hold them back. She told herself she must be getting better. After all, she hadn't cried in almost ten hours. Now, if only she could do something about the raw pain in her chest—in the place where her heart had been before Tristan had taken it with him.

LIZ AND HOLLY SHOWED UP on Devon's doorstep that evening, unannounced. Liz carried two large, hot pizzas heaped with toppings; Holly bore two bottles of wine. "We decided you need company tonight," Holly declared, breezing through the door with her coppery ponytail bobbing defiantly behind her. "Gonna throw us out?"

Devon smiled. "You know I won't. Come on in."

"This was Holly's idea," Liz defended herself. "But I decided she was probably right."

"I'm glad you're here," Devon admitted. "Both of you," she added with a fond glance at Holly.

"Then lead us to the kitchen," Holly ordered gaily. "I'm starving and the smell of that pizza is about to drive me to violence."

Devon glanced at her watch with a frown. "It's almost time for Tristan's first evening report," she said.

"We'll have a bedroom-floor picnic and watch it together," Liz suggested. "You get a tablecloth and Holly will get wineglasses. I have to put these pizzas down before my arms drop off."

Ten minutes later the three friends sat in front of the television set in Devon's bedroom—a green-and-white checkered cloth spread on the floor, and pizza, paper plates and napkins scattered over it. A silver ice bucket held the wine, and three pairs of shoes were strewn carelessly around it.

"This reminds me of the slumber parties I used to have as a kid," Holly commented, her mouth decorated with a dot of pizza sauce. She licked it off when she finished speaking.

"You had wine at your slumber parties?" Devon asked, motioning with her half-empty glass.

Holly giggled. "Actually, we used to sneak in beer. I hated the stuff, so I never made it through an entire can. I still can't get it past my nose. One sniff and I start shuddering."

"My friends and I had a slumber party the week before graduation," Liz reminisced with a mischievous smile. "We got smashed on rum and cola. We spent most of the night throwing up and then were all grounded for the remainder of the week. My parents were furious with me, but Neal thought it was funny, even though he gave me a long, big-brother lecture about mature behavior and the dangers of alcohol. I assured him that I hadn't found anything all that appealing about being thoroughly, disgustingly sick and waking up with a headache the size of a bus."

"At my last slumber party we had popcorn and hot chocolate," Devon mused. "*Wuthering Heights* was on the late show that night and we watched it from our sleeping bags and then discussed the differences between the book and the movie before going to sleep."

"A real wild night, huh?" Holly teased.

"Mmm. It was a birthday party for the president of the Honor Society. She was my best friend during high school. She's a defense attorney in Boston now. Harvard graduate." Devon looked thoughtfully at the wineglass in her hand. "I was a senior in college before I had my first taste of alcohol. I've never been intoxicated. I was twenty-two when I went to bed with Wade, after he and I had been engaged for three months. During the two years we were engaged, I think we spent maybe a dozen nights together."

Liz wiped her mouth with a paper napkin. "Are you sorry you didn't choose a wilder life-style?" she asked matter-of-factly.

Devon met her friend's understanding eyes with a slight smile. "Not anymore," she replied quietly. "I know now that a quiet, traditional life is exactly right for me. I enjoy simple pleasures—like having pizza with you guys tonight. Visiting my mom and grandmother on Sunday afternoons. Walking in the park. Good books, soft music, romantic movies. Brandy would be bored to tears, but I don't believe she's any happier than I have been."

Liz raise her glass in a salute, her engagement ring glinting with the movement. "Here's to the good life," she said. "Family, friends and successful careers."

Holly nodded, then sighed deeply. "You, at least, have Chance," she reminded Liz. "I have the friends and career, but I'd like a family, too." The only offspring of a couple she claimed had been the inspiration for every old television-family program, Holly made no secret of her longing to have children of her own. At twenty-five, she was determined to see that dream come true. Her only problem, she complained, was that she was one of those conservative types who thought marriage should come before children. And she refused to marry a man she didn't love.

Devon's heart twisted as she agreed silently with Holly. All her life needed was someone to share it with, she thought longingly. And the only man she wanted might have been driven away by her own blind stupidity.

As though in response to her thoughts, Tristan's name sounded from the television set. Devon immediately snatched up the remote control to raise the volume.

"Earlier today, Tristan Parrish taped the following report from a compound in which the families of rebel troops are living in conditions of grim desperation. We're showing you the tape as we received it, unedited. We warn you that some of the sights you will see will be disturbing."

And then Tristan was on-screen, his handsome face grave, etched deeply with weariness and reaction to the suffering he'd seen during the past two weeks. Lethargic women, children and elderly sat in the crude encampment surrounding him, staring at the foreign film crew with blank, hollow eyes. Tristan's voice was gravelly as he filed his report about the progress of the bloody insurrection, then went on to describe the atrocities being leveled at the families and supporters of the rebels.

Kneeling beside a mewling toddler with near-skeletal limbs and a grotesquely bloated stomach, cloudy eyes and cracked lips, Tristan explained that months of severe drought and governmental greediness had robbed the poor populace of food and supplies, leaving them to die of illness and starvation.

"Listless children like this one lie starving on filthy, fly-teeming pallets ... while the food that could save them rots in government-controlled warehouses," Tristan said, obviously struggling to hold on to his objectivity. Devon watched with a lump in her throat as the man she loved reached out to touch the child's dirty, sore-spotted back. She wondered if anyone who didn't know him so well would have heard the emotional break in his voice. He'd covered it quickly and professionally, but Devon knew he was hurting. And her eyes filled with tears for him.

Liz reached out and took Devon's hand, holding it in both of her own. Devon clung gratefully to the silent support.

The taped report came to an abrupt end when cameras cut back to the desk where the middle-aged, gray-haired anchor looked up from a sheet of paper before him. "This just in," he announced. "Rebel leaders have been captured and a government spokesman claims that the attempted coup has failed. The populace is in turmoil and marshal law has been declared. All foreign journalists have been advised to leave the country immediately. We are not in contact with our crew at this time, but they have been given instructions to leave at once. We'll keep you informed as to their progress. The President announced today that . . ."

"Oh, God," Devon murmured, closing her eyes tightly as she issued a fervent prayer for Tristan's safety. "Oh, please."

"He'll be okay, Devon," Liz said firmly. "Tristan's been in tight spots before. He knows how to take care of himself."

Devon opened her eyes and took a deep breath. "I know. It's just—" Her voice trailed away.

Her own eyes deeply troubled, Liz nodded. "Yes. I know. I'm worried about him, too."

Her hands tightened around Devon's. "Look, Devon, I don't know exactly what happened between you and Tristan, but I know you wouldn't have gone to Serendipity Island with him if you hadn't cared about him. And I know that something went wrong when you returned—something you haven't even been able to talk about yet. I'm not trying to pry. I just want you to know that if you need me, I'm here." She glanced at Holly. "We're both here," she added.

"I know," Devon whispered. "And it means so much to me to have you for my friends. I wish I could explain, but—" But how could she, when she herself wasn't exactly sure what had gone wrong that last night? She only knew that Tristan had looked angry and hurt when he'd left—so angry and so hurt that she wasn't sure she'd ever see him again. Not by his choice, anyway.

And she wasn't sure she'd ever find the nerve to force the confrontation herself. And what if she'd been wrong? What if he'd decided later that he was actually relieved that it had ended so quickly, so thoroughly? Or, what if he'd never felt more for her than the casual interest she'd assumed from the beginning?

"You know, Devon, I don't have anything pressing waiting for me at home," Holly commented. "I could stay with you tonight, if you want. We can wait for news together."

"Oh, Holly, thank you for offering, but it's really not necessary," Devon assured her. "I don't think I'd be very good company. I'll be fine, really."

It was very obvious that softhearted Holly couldn't stand to see Devon in such pain. "You really love him a lot, don't you?" she asked sympathetically.

"Yes. I do." It was the first time Devon had ever acknowledged her feelings for Tristan to anyone but herself.

"Maybe it will work out," Liz offered. "Neal said that he'd never seen Tristan as taken with any woman as he was with you. Neal thought it was getting pretty serious."

Wearily blinking back those ever-threatening tears, Devon shook her head. "If it was, Tristan never let me know."

"Did you ever tell him how *you* felt?" Liz asked gently.

"No," Devon admitted sadly. "I never did."

Tristan had left thinking Devon had been indulging herself in a "pleasant fling." Yet he'd claimed to know her so well. Didn't he understand that it had always been more than that for her, no matter what she'd so stupidly said to Brandy? Could she ever make him believe differently? Or had she even crossed his mind since he'd driven away?

The twenty-four-hour news station announced the successful evacuation of their crew at three forty-five Saturday morning, Devon's time. She hadn't slept at all since Liz and Holly had left hours earlier. Instead, she'd sat propped against her bed pillows, trying to read a book as she kept half her attention turned to the television.

She sagged in weary relief as a live broadcast showed Tristan and his co-workers stepping off a plane in Cairo, along with the other journalism crews who'd been evacuated at the same time. "Thank God," she whispered, her voice hoarse with worry and lack of sleep. Only then did she allow herself to rest, but she slept fitfully for what little remained of the night.

Tristan was safe, she told herself when she awoke, heavy eyed, achy and empty. Nothing was more important to her than that.

12

TRISTAN GLANCED broodingly at his calendar watch and noted the date. Saturday, February 29. Leap years always irritated him. There'd been twenty-eight days of February for the past three years and now there was this other day tacked on. And what about those poor unfortunates born on this date? How the hell did they know when to celebrate for the next three years?

He sighed deeply and dropped his arm. He didn't really care about the date, he thought wearily. He was just trying, as usual, to think about anything other than Devon.

He roamed restlessly around his house, the afternoon and evening ahead packed with too many empty hours. At least for the past month he'd been able to keep himself busy, dashing from one assignment to another, spending no more than one night at a time in Atlanta—just long enough to pack fresh clothes and head out again. His choice. He'd begged, cajoled and demanded every new story that had come along to keep him on the move, keep his thoughts occupied with other people's problems rather than his own pain.

At least this time no one was threatening to tie him to a hospital bed. He was tired, yes, but he'd taken care to eat right and get plenty of rest, determined that concerns for his health wouldn't earn him another unwanted holiday. He was in better shape than in a long time—physically. Emotionally—Well, that was another story.

If only he could stop remembering how good he and Devon had been together, how right it had felt to be with her. How special he'd thought they were. He'd been thinking "forever," marriage and children, and she'd been prepared all along for the end.

"Tristan and I have had fun, but that's all there is to it. What makes you think I'd even want more than that from him?"

He groaned as the words echoed again in his mind, and remembered all too well the others that followed them.

"What woman wouldn't enjoy a pleasant little fling on a tropical island with a fascinating man?"

Even if Devon had been hiding her real feelings from her sister when she'd said those things, Brandy hadn't been around when Tristan had asked, *"Tell me, Devon, whatever made you think that all I wanted from you was an affair—a fling?"*

"I've always known," she had answered as though surprised by the question. *"Everyone knows that you're not interested in anything more serious, that you aren't interested in commitments."*

He'd thought his family's lack of belief in him had hurt so many years earlier. But hearing Devon say that she had never expected him to be anything more to her than a temporary sexual partner had shattered him.

He'd never known anything could hurt this badly.

He lifted his head warily when his doorbell chimed. He wasn't expecting anyone. Few people even knew he was back in town. Did Devon? Even if she did, the chances were slim to none that she was the one at his door, he decided. More likely some kid selling magazines. He should just ignore it.

But then he decided what the hell. He was in the mood to chew raw meat, anyway. Sending a solicitor packing would be almost as satisfying.

His vicious mood softened immediately when he found Neal Archer on his doorstep. "Neal! Come in."

"Got a beer?" Neal asked, stepping past Tristan into the entryway.

"Of course. It's entirely possible that I even have pretzels to go with it."

"Sounds good. You get the food, I'll find a ball game on TV. Meet you in the den."

Rather bemused by Neal's unexpected visit and brusque manner, Tristan complied.

Carrying a tray into the den, he found Neal lounging comfortably on the deep sofa, his shoes kicked off and his feet propped on the round table in front of him. Neal was apparently already involved in the basketball game playing on the large-screen television set.

"So what's up, Neal?" he inquired when they were both comfortable, beer cans in hand, bowls of pretzels at their elbows.

"Sara's off somewhere with Phillip and I've caught up with work for a change, so I thought I'd come over and hassle you for a while. You know how I get when I'm bored."

"Mmm. This from the man who's supposedly looking forward to living alone for the first time in his life?" Tristan asked skeptically.

Neal grinned and shrugged. "I guess it'll take some getting used to."

They watched the game in silence for a few minutes, Tristan waiting patiently until Neal decided it was time to bring up whatever had prompted his visit this afternoon. It wasn't that Neal hadn't shown up unannounced before, just as Tristan had made occasional impulsive visits to Neal's home. But he knew his friend well enough to see that Neal had something on his mind.

It didn't take long. "You rested up from that last assignment yet? Covering a hurricane in the Philippines is no easy task, is it?"

"I'm not going to collapse again, if that's what you're trying to determine. I didn't exactly brave the winds and waves, Neal. I only reported on the aftermath."

"In weather almost as vicious as the storm had been," Neal reminded him.

Tristan shrugged. "I've seen worse."

"Yes, I know you have. You didn't put your life in danger even once for this story. You must be slipping."

"Knock it off, Neal."

"Well, now you've been home almost twenty-four hours. Have you called Devon yet?"

Tristan's fingers tightened around his beer can. "No."

"Going to?"

"No."

"Why not?"

From anyone else, Tristan would have considered the question prying. But this was Neal. Neal, who knew exactly how serious Tristan had been about Devon. "I don't think she'd be interested."

"I find that hard to believe. Liz and Sara think Devon's been hurting since you left town. If she looks as grim as you do, they're probably right."

Tristan snorted his disbelief, sternly quashing a faint flicker of hope. "Why should Devon be hurt by my leaving? After all, she fully expected it from the beginning. Everyone knows I'm not the type to hang around for long. Right?"

Neal pushed a button on the remote control, leaving the game playing on without sound. And then he turned to Tristan. "Want to talk about it?"

Surprisingly enough, he did. All of it—from the moment Sara had introduced them, to the next day when Tristan had seen Devon in the wedding gown. He even told Neal about consoling himself with too many beers during Neal's date with Devon, only to appear on her doorstep later that evening in an embarrassingly intoxicated condition. He talked about the luncheon he'd arranged for her, Devon's touching reaction to it. About movies and wallpaper, laughter and dancing. About four and a half days in paradise.

And then he told Neal exactly what Devon had said to Brandy, and to Tristan afterward. Neal listened to the entire story without a word, his expression gratifyingly sympathetic. Tristan fully expected Neal to be loyally outraged by Devon's behavior. Instead, Neal only nodded once when Tristan finished, took a long swig of his beer and remarked, "You really made a mess of it this time, didn't you, friend?"

Jolted, Tristan stared at Neal. "*I* made a mess of it?"

Neal nodded and finished his beer.

"Neal, weren't you listening to anything I said? I was falling in love with her, damn it! Devon's the one who thought we were just having an amusing little affair."

"And how was she supposed to know differently?" Neal asked calmly. "You've talked about wining and dining her, about romancing her, but you haven't said a word about telling her the way you felt about her. Did you ever let her know how you felt? Did you ever once say that you wanted a future with her?"

Remembering Rafe's unheeded advice, Tristan shifted uncomfortably. "Well, not in so many words," he admitted. "I was trying to give her time to know me, to determine her own feelings about me."

"She had two entire weeks," Neal agreed with a nod. "And in all that time she never learned to read your mind? Kind of slow, isn't she?"

"Dammit, Neal—"

"For that matter, you had two whole weeks to get to know Devon. Tell me, Tristan, does she seem like the type who'd jet off to the Caribbean with a near stranger for an 'amusing little affair'? Funny, she struck me as the type who'd have to care a great deal for a man before she'd get that deeply involved with him."

"I would have said that about her, too—until I heard her talking to Brandy."

"Isn't it possible that Devon was protecting herself from disappointment because you never let her know you wanted more from her than you had?"

Tristan scowled. "She should have known," he muttered.

"Ah. So you *did* expect her to read your mind."

Flushing, Tristan cursed beneath his breath. "I'm not good at expressing my feelings. You know that. And I have a lot of old scars that make me a bit sensitive about being misjudged."

"Well, I'll tell you, Tristan," Neal said curtly, shoving himself to his feet in apparent preparation for departure, "unless you want to lose Devon forever, you'd better get your butt over to her house to explain why you're so damned sensitive and why you never told her she was more to you than a fling between assignments."

Setting his own half-finished drink on the coffee table, Tristan rose, as well. "You don't understand, Neal."

Neal's gray eyes softened. "I understand, Tristan. I understand that you're hurting worse than I've ever seen you. I don't like it."

Tristan shrugged ruefully. "Neither do I."

Neal cuffed his arm. "Then do something about it, buddy. I gave you your shot with this woman, you know. Don't blow it."

"Yeah," Tristan responded with a weak attempt at humor. "Like you ever had a chance once she'd met me."

"I don't know," Neal replied, heading for the front door. "Looks to me like you tried to give her back on a silver platter. Devon's a special woman. You're just damned lucky I didn't decide to try my luck again."

Devon, Tristan thought with a sheepish smile, would have both their heads on a silver platter if she heard them talking about her like a rare collectible the two men were negotiating over. Which, of course, led to inevitable reflections upon the misconceptions one might receive from eavesdropping on private conversations.

Listening to the sound of Neal's car leaving the driveway, Tristan stood motionless in his foyer, wondering if Neal had been right. Had Devon been protecting herself from wanting more than she thought Tristan was willing to give? Had Tristan lost her because he'd let old pride and old hurts come between them? Or was there still hope for them, if only Tristan was willing to take the risk of being hurt yet again?

The man who'd been applauded so many times for his courage in the face of danger suddenly found himself afraid of facing one slim, beautiful woman who held the rest of his life in her small, soft hands.

DEVON'S DOORBELL RANG at ten o'clock Saturday evening. She looked up with a start from the pile of order forms spread in front of her. The last time she'd been summoned to the door at such a late hour, she'd found Tristan on the other side, ridiculously charming and intoxicated.

Her throat tightened. Could it be—?

Her arms crossed tightly over her soft silk-and-angora knit sweater, she took a deep breath as she stepped close to the door. "Who is it?"

"It's Tristan. I know it's late, but . . ."

She had the door open before he finished the sentence. "Tristan."

Hungrily she searched his face, finding the faint signs of fatigue, wariness—apprehension? She stepped back. "Come in."

Hands buried in the pockets of his black leather jacket, he stepped past her—and then stood looking around him as if wondering why he was there. She closed the door, then turned to face him, nervously still clutching the doorknob behind her.

Tristan cleared his throat and glanced at her. "I suppose you'd like to know why I'm here."

"The question had crossed my mind," she admitted huskily.

"I'm not drunk," he assured her quickly.

She smiled, despite her tension. "I know."

Sighing deeply, Tristan shook his head. "I'm making a mess of this."

Dropping her hands, Devon took a step closer, sensing he needed help. "Why don't you take off your jacket and get comfortable," she suggested practically. "Can I get you something to drink?"

"No, thanks." But he shrugged out of his jacket and tossed it aside, which left him clad in a hunter-green sweater and dark gray slacks. Devon thought he looked wonderful, but a few pounds thinner than when she'd last seen him.

Tristan motioned toward the couch. "We need to talk, Devon."

She nodded, but rather than sitting beside him on the sofa she chose a nearby wing chair where she could watch his face. "What did you want to talk about?"

Sitting stiffly on the couch, he crossed his legs, then uncrossed them, his hands folding, then clenching. His uncharacteristic fidgeting made Devon even more curious about his reason for being there. She laced her fingers together against a sudden urge to reach out to him. Her love for him hadn't lessened in the weeks since she'd last seen him. If anything, she loved him more now than she had when he'd left. She'd had five long, lonely, painful weeks of missing him.

"There was something I should have told you the night before I left for Africa," Tristan began abruptly. "I shouldn't have left without telling you how you hurt me by the things I heard you telling your sister."

"Can—" Her voice came out little more than a croak. Her throat had tightened again at his raw admission that she had, indeed, hurt him. She tried again. "Can you tell me now?"

"I'll try," he said. "But this is very difficult for me. I haven't talked about my past to anyone in a very long time. Neal knows some of what happened, but not all. I want you to know it all."

Devon caught her breath. "But why—?"

He held up a hand to silence her, his eyes dark, his expression unreadable. "Just hear me out, okay?"

She bit her lip and motioned for him to proceed.

He took a deep breath. "I told you that I come from an old, distinguished family line."

She nodded again. "Your father was a baron," she whispered, remembering every word he'd said about his family. Remembering that he'd furiously accused her of being just like them.

"Yes. A very respectable, quite unreproachable baron. My older brother, Charles, is exactly like my father. He was perfect from the moment of his birth, a credit to the family name. My sister, Honoria, was the most virtuous, admirable daughter any family could ever desire. And then there was me."

Devon remembered that he'd phrased it that way before, calling himself the "ne'er-do-well younger son." Her heart twisted at the bitterness in his voice.

"I was never what they wanted, never what they expected. Everything I attempted somehow went wrong. I tried for years to please them, to live up to their expectations. And then I grew tired of trying. They always expected the worst from me, and eventually that's exactly what they got."

"Oh, Tristan. I'm sorry."

He shook his head to indicate that he wasn't finished. "When I was twenty-two, I finally made my family happy. I became engaged to a woman they'd hand selected for me almost from my birth, the daughter of a family whose lands adjoined ours. Sounds like an old novel, doesn't it?" he added, his smile utterly without humor.

"Did you love her?" Devon asked quietly, though she already knew the answer.

"No, I didn't," Tristan replied, his voice flat, tired. "But I thought I'd try one last time to please my family. Everything was fine at first—and then I met Anna."

Devon tensed. "Anna?"

His eyes grew sad. "She was nineteen and funny and outgoing. Always laughing, very affectionate and demonstrative. Everything my fiancée, Evelyn, was not. I don't know if I loved Anna, but I was enthralled by her. Perhaps I would have grown to love her, had we been given the chance. I tried desperately to remind myself that I was engaged, that I had no business seeing another woman. And I swear that I did nothing more than kiss her one time when I could no longer resist. Unfortunately, it happened in the garden of my fiancée's family home on the night of our engagement party. And that, of course, was the moment my fiancée discovered us."

"Oh, no."

"Oh, yes. She became hysterical. Her family was infuriated, my own mortified. In front of everyone we knew, my father denounced me as a worthless playboy who'd been carrying on an affair right under his dear, innocent fiancée's nose. He told me that he had given up on trying to mold me into a worthy adult, that he had no further use for me from that moment. Anna was so humiliated that she refused to ever see me again. She left the next day to spend time with family members in France. My engagement, of course, was over."

Devon's eyes stung with tears she refused to shed. "When did you leave?"

He shrugged. "Two, maybe three weeks later, when the silent disapproval finally grew too unbearable. My father told me he hoped I'd make less a mess of my life in America than I had in England. My mother cried, but never asked me to change my mind. My brother and sister seemed relieved that I wouldn't be around to embarrass them further with their crowd."

"Did you know anyone here? Was there anyone to welcome you?"

"No. I arrived quite by myself, with only a small inheritance from my maternal grandfather to live on until I found a job. I had a university degree in journalism, so I talked myself onto a newspaper staff in New York. I showed considerable aptitude for the job and took advantage of every opportunity to move up. I answered an ad for a newspaper reporter in Atlanta almost five years after I'd arrived in the States and I've been here ever since."

Devon wanted to know how he'd made the change from newspaper to television reporting, but at the moment that wasn't nearly as important as other questions. Why had he come here tonight to tell her these things? What did his conflict with his family have to do with his relationship with her?

As though he'd read her thoughts, Tristan leaned slightly forward, looking at her intently. "Since I left England, I suppose I've tried my best to live up to my family's low opinion of me. I've lived recklessly and improvidently, avoiding commitments and responsibilities, risking everything for fame and awards, as though I had to prove something to myself, as well as to them. Maybe I thought I didn't really deserve a home and family because I'd screwed up so royally the first time I tried. And then I met you."

His voice grew husky. "I thought I'd been given a reprieve—a chance to have it all. To be the man I'd always wanted to be in the eyes of someone who looked inside me and saw the real Tristan Parrish, not the public facade. And then I heard you talking to Brandy and I realized that your opinion of me was little better than my family's or that of others who think of me as nothing more than an irresponsible libertine who uses women as temporary playthings before moving on in search of fresh prey."

Stricken, Devon held out a beseeching hand. "Tristan, no. It wasn't that way. I didn't—"

"Didn't you?" he broke in heavily, still holding her gaze with his own.

The words hit her like a slap. Hadn't that been exactly what she'd thought of him? Hadn't that been the reason she'd steeled herself against wanting too much from him; the reason she'd thought from the beginning that he would soon grow tired of her and leave her in search of new adventure, new challenges? Hadn't she thought him the perfect "bad boy" with whom to shed her "good girl" image?

She'd misjudged him so horribly. And, in doing so, she'd lost him. But why had he come back, after she'd hurt him so deeply? "Tristan," she whispered, her eyes filling. "I'm so sorry."

He swallowed and reached for her hand, cradling it in his own. "It wasn't your fault, Devon. It was mine. I never told you how I felt. I never gave you reason to believe I wanted anything more than we had. I was so smugly certain that you knew exactly what I wanted that I neglected to give you the words. For a man who makes his living in communications, that was a stupid, careless error in judgment.

"I know I didn't give you much time to get to know me," he added swiftly when she would have spoken. His fingers tightened around hers. "I know I shouldn't have expected so much from you so quickly. I'd like to know now if it's too late to start over—to show you that I'm capable of changing, that I have so much to offer you if you'll only give me the opportunity to prove it. I've loved you from the beginning, Devon. Please give me a chance to teach you to love me, too."

Her tears spilled onto her cheeks as she slid from the chair and knelt in front of him, both her hands held tightly in his own. "Oh, Tristan, you don't have to prove anything to me," she whispered, her breath catching. "I know what a wonderful man you are. I foolishly let my own fears and insecurities, my own past mistakes blind me for a time, but I've always known the truth deep inside. I loved you so much that I went too far in trying to protect myself against being hurt if you didn't feel the same way about me."

He rose to his feet, pulling her with him. "You love me?" he asked hoarsely, as if he wasn't quite sure he'd heard correctly.

"From the first," she answered fervently. "But I was so busy preparing for the end that I didn't give us a real chance at a beginning. Can you ever forgive me for hurting you that way?"

"Devon." He pulled her into his arms, his face buried in her hair. "Oh, my love, I'll forgive you anything if only you'll tell me again that you love me."

"I do. Tristan, I love you so much."

He crushed her mouth beneath his, just as she reached up to lock her arms around his neck.

IT WAS WELL AFTER midnight and yet Devon and Tristan were still awake, lying close together in her bed, still pleasantly dazed by their newly professed love for each other. Tristan couldn't seem to stop touching her, finding it hard to believe that after all those weeks of lonely misery, he'd had only to reach out to her to have her in his arms again.

He didn't know that he deserved such happiness, but he vowed to spend the rest of his life proving himself worthy of Devon's love. Which reminded him . . .

"Devon?"

She stirred contentedly in his arms. "Mmm?"

He cleared his throat. "I know it's too soon to bring this up. I mean, we've really only known each other a few weeks, and we've spent most of those apart. And I did promise to give you time to get to know me."

She lifted her head to look at him. "What is it, Tristan?"

God, she was so beautiful. He cupped her cheek in one near-reverent hand. "I just want you to know that I will never stop loving you. That my commitment to you is permanent and exclusive. And that, as soon as you're ready to take such a great step, I want you to be my wife. I know it's too early to expect an answer now, but—"

"I'll marry you tomorrow, if that's what you want."

The quiet certainty in her words took his breath away. "You're sure?" he asked anxiously. "You're not being impulsive or—or carried away by passion?"

She smiled at his phrasing and leaned over to kiss him. "My darling Tristan, I have wanted to marry you since the day you first walked through my door. And I have definitely been carried away by passion—and I hope to be again. Soon."

Tristan knew he'd never been happier in his life. He also knew that no matter how much joy lay ahead for him, he'd never forget this one perfect moment when the woman he loved agreed to risk joining her future with his. "You're a demanding woman, Devon Fleming."

She laughed wickedly and pressed another kiss to his lips. "Consider yourself warned, my love."

Laughing, he tumbled her beneath him and loomed over her. "One more thing."

She slid one hand up his chest and around to the back of his neck and her legs tangled with his. "Make it fast."

"It's about my job."

She went still beneath him, teasing forgotten for the moment. "What about your job?"

"I'm considering a change. Something that won't involve so much traveling. I've several offers to consider, but of course I'd like to discuss them with you first."

"That really isn't necessary, Tristan. I mean, I'd love to have you here all the time, if possible, but I'd never ask you to give up reporting for me," she assured him. "I have my own career to keep me busy, and I'd be perfectly happy knowing you'll always come home to me when your assignments are over."

"But I would be perfectly miserable spending so much time away from you," he returned soberly. "I don't want to be a part-time husband—or a part-time father. I'm ready to settle down, to try new challenges. I want a home, Devon. A real one."

"Oh, Tristan," she whispered, pulling him closer. "I love you."

Tristan kissed her tenderly, sealing the promises they'd made. Devon loved him. Devon believed in him. And all he'd had to do was ask, he thought in amazement—to take a risk at making himself vulnerable, exposing his true feelings.

He made a mental note to thank Rafe and Neal for such valuable advice. He'd ask them to stand as groomsmen for his wedding, he decided contentedly, then promptly forgot them both as Devon's hand closed lovingly around him.

At the moment, he had much more urgent emotions to express.

Epilogue

A CAMERA CLICKED as Devon stood still for her mother to adjust her wedding veil. She realized that another precious moment leading up to her wedding had just been captured on film, and turned to Holly with a smile. "You're very sneaky," she accused. "I didn't even know you were there this time."

Holly grinned. "That's why I'm the best," she quipped.

"Oh, Devon, this dress is so beautiful," Alice sighed, her eyes tear-filled. "The most beautiful one you've ever designed, I think."

"Thanks, Mom." Devon looked down at the dress and thought of the look on Tristan's face the first time he'd seen her in it. It was hard to remember that it had ever been meant for anyone else. In her heart she believed that fate had intended it to be hers all along. Tristan had agreed, telling her that he couldn't imagine her wearing another gown, however beautiful it might be.

"I still wish Tristan hadn't seen your dress before," her grandmother fretted, carefully clutching Devon's bouquet. "It's bad luck, you know."

Devon only laughed. "Trust me, Grammie. With this gown, the opposite must be true. If Tristan hadn't seen me wearing it that day everything might have been different."

Plucking impatiently at her own pale peach organza dress, Brandy sighed. "This really isn't my style, you know, Dev? It's just too . . . ruffly."

"Why, Brandy, you look lovely!" Alice chided. "The dress is perfect for an April wedding. You'll look like a breath of spring walking down the aisle."

Brandy made a face at her mother's "old-fashioned" description. Devon only smiled. Nothing could spoil this day for her—not even Brandy's complaints.

"And here's the maid of honor," Holly announced, aiming her camera at the door as Liz entered. The peach gown made a perfect foil for Liz's fair coloring. Devon had known it would be when she'd chosen the color for her attendants.

"I still wish there'd been a way to have you as a bridesmaid and yet have you take my wedding pictures," Devon told Holly regretfully. "You know I'd have liked you up there beside me."

"I'll be there," Holly promised with a smile. She held up her camera. "And you'll always have the photographs to prove it." Holly's services—and several albums full of beautiful photographs—would be her wedding gift to Devon and Tristan. After all, no one else could have recorded her wedding as lovingly or as sensitively as Holly.

"The ceremony is about to begin," Liz announced to the women crowding the little dressing room. "Is everyone ready? Devon?"

"More than ready," Devon assured her. "Liz, you've worked magic getting all this together so quickly for me."

Liz laughed. "I doubt that Tristan could have waited another week for this wedding. I didn't think any man could be more impatient to get married than Chance, but he and Tristan are closely tied."

"They both know how lucky they are," Holly asserted loyally. "Neither wants to take a chance on something going wrong."

"Not a chance," Devon said firmly at the same time Liz added, "No way." And then they laughed sheepishly at their sentimental happiness. Holly sighed with visible envy. Devon's mother and grandmother smiled and wiped at their eyes. Brandy just looked bored.

The traditional ceremony began flawlessly. Devon's mother and grandmother were seated, candles lit, solos sung. Devon waited patiently in the church foyer while a tiny cousin dropped rose petals down the aisle, followed by Brandy and then Liz. The music swelled, the many guests rose, and it was Devon's turn. She entered alone, wishing for a moment that her father had lived to give her away. And then she saw Tristan waiting for her—tall and golden and so very handsome in his formal clothing—and even the most fleeting of regrets vanished. How could she ask for anything more than this?

When her eyes locked with Tristan's, she was only dimly aware of the crowded sanctuary, of Liz and Brandy waiting for her to take her place beside them, of Neal and Rafe watching Tristan's eagerness with indulgent smiles.

At last Tristan's hand, warm and steady was around hers. His smile was loving, tender, utterly confident. "I love you," he murmured.

"I love you," she whispered in return, happily confident that they would never again hesitate to share their deepest feelings.

HARLEQUIN®

Don't miss these Harlequin favorites by some of our most distinguished authors!
And now, you can receive a discount by ordering two or more titles!

HT #25645	THREE GROOMS AND A WIFE by JoAnn Ross	$3.25 U.S./$3.75 CAN. ☐
HT #25648	JESSIE'S LAWMAN by Kristine Rolofson	$3.25 U.S.//$3.75 CAN. ☐
HP #11725	THE WRONG KIND OF WIFE by Roberta Leigh	$3.25 U.S./$3.75 CAN. ☐
HP #11755	TIGER EYES by Robyn Donald	$3.25 U.S./$3.75 CAN. ☐
HR #03362	THE BABY BUSINESS by Rebecca Winters	$2.99 U.S./$3.50 CAN. ☐
HR #03375	THE BABY CAPER by Emma Goldrick	$2.99 U.S./$3.50 CAN. ☐
HS #70638	THE SECRET YEARS by Margot Dalton	$3.75 U.S./$4.25 CAN. ☐
HS #70655	PEACEKEEPER by Marisa Carroll	$3.75 U.S./$4.25 CAN. ☐
HI #22280	MIDNIGHT RIDER by Laura Pender	$2.99 U.S./$3.50 CAN. ☐
HI #22235	BEAUTY VS THE BEAST by M.J. Rogers	$3.50 U.S./$3.99 CAN. ☐
HAR #16531	TEDDY BEAR HEIR by Elda Minger	$3.50 U.S./$3.99 CAN. ☐
HAR #16596	COUNTERFEIT HUSBAND by Linda Randall Wisdom	$3.50 U.S./$3.99 CAN. ☐
HH #28795	PIECES OF SKY by Marianne Willman	$3.99 U.S./$4.50 CAN. ☐
HH #28855	SWEET SURRENDER by Julie Tetel	$4.50 U.S./$4.99 CAN. ☐

(limited quantities available on certain titles)

	AMOUNT	$
DEDUCT:	10% DISCOUNT FOR 2+ BOOKS	$
ADD:	POSTAGE & HANDLING	$
	($1.00 for one book, 50¢ for each additional)	
	APPLICABLE TAXES**	$_____
	TOTAL PAYABLE	$_____
	(check or money order—please do not send cash)	

To order, complete this form and send it, along with a check or money order for the total above, payable to Harlequin Books, to: **In the U.S.:** 3010 Walden Avenue, P.O. Box 9047, Buffalo, NY 14269-9047; **In Canada:** P.O. Box 613, Fort Erie, Ontario, L2A 5X3.

Name: _____

Address: _____ City: _____

State/Prov.: _____ Zip/Postal Code: _____

**New York residents remit applicable sales taxes.
Canadian residents remit applicable GST and provincial taxes.   HBACK-AJ3

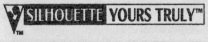

▼ Silhouette ROMANCE™

What's a single dad to do when he needs a wife by next Thursday?

Who's a confirmed bachelor to call when he finds a baby on his doorstep?

How does a plain Jane in love with her gorgeous boss get him to notice her?

From classic love stories to romantic comedies to emotional heart tuggers, **Silhouette Romance** offers six irresistible novels every month by some of your favorite authors!
Such as...beloved bestsellers **Diana Palmer,**
Annette Broadrick, Suzanne Carey, Elizabeth August
and **Marie Ferrarella,** to name just a few—and some sure to become favorites!

Fabulous Fathers...Bundles of Joy...Miniseries...
Months of blushing brides and convenient weddings...
Holiday celebrations... You'll find all this and much more in
Silhouette Romance—always emotional, always enjoyable, always about love!

SR-GEN

Harlequin Romance ®

Delightful

Affectionate

Romantic

Emotional

Tender

Original

Daring

Riveting

Enchanting

Adventurous

Moving

Harlequin Romance—the
series that has it all!

HROM-G

◈ Harlequin®
◈ Historical

If you're a serious fan of historical romance,
then you're in luck!

Harlequin Historicals brings you
stories by bestselling authors, rising new stars
and talented first-timers.

Ruth Langan & Theresa Michaels
Mary McBride & Cheryl St. John
Margaret Moore & Merline Lovelace
Julie Tetel & Nina Beaumont
Susan Amarillas & Ana Seymour
Deborah Simmons & Linda Castle
Cassandra Austin & Emily French
Miranda Jarrett & Suzanne Barclay
DeLoras Scott & Laurie Grant...

You'll never run out of favorites.

Harlequin Historicals...they're too good to miss!

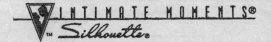

Elvis Presley
and
Priscilla Beaulieu

Elvis was introduced to Priscilla by an army buddy while stationed in Germany. She was fourteen. She visited Elvis at Graceland in 1960. About a year later, her family agreed to allow her to move to Memphis and finish high school at Immaculate Conception.

After Priscilla turned twenty-one, Colonel Tom Parker (Elvis's manager and promoter) insisted they get married. Elvis proposed on Christmas Eve 1966.

They were married in the Aladdin Hotel with an eight-minute ceremony by Judge Zenoff. Exactly nine months later Lisa Marie was born.

Elvis fans have always claimed the spelling of his middle name "Aaron" is wrong. He spelled it "Aron." Supposedly Elvis legally changed it, and a recording label called Aaron Records, from his middle name, was begun in the late fifties. However, when Elvis filled out his marriage application in 1967, he clearly wrote in his own hand "Elvis Aron Presley."

B-ELVIS